I0536623

THE GAMBLERS

by

DIANA PHILBRICK

Published by **CHIMERA**
ISBN 9781780807942

CHAPTER ONE

The style was called 'Anguish'. It was the latest fashion rage - dress your woman in haute-couture, bind her in some minor way, and then hurt her... just a little... just enough to draw out her beauty. It looked sophisticated when it was done properly, with a light touch.

This definitely was not the case for the contract-girl across the aisle. Her look simply wasn't working. She was just a CELT of course, which allowed for a more daring presentation, but even so, one could only get away with so much skin, so much pain. In my opinion, the mark of a real sophisticate was subtlety.

Not that this girl wasn't beautiful, quite the contrary, she was extraordinary - light brown skin, a face that could launch ships, shoulder-length chestnut hair, a long graceful neck; and tall, maybe five-ten, with an athlete's perfectly sculpted body, one that came with hard, consistent exercise. Someone had really worked this girl to get such a figure.

It was difficult to nail down exactly what was wrong with her look though. Every part of her presentation was correct if slightly overdone; maybe that was it; maybe it was all just too much.

Pleased with my sudden insight, I studied her more closely over the top of my computer. She was sitting back on her heels, wearing a white sundress. This was his first mistake - a sexy sundress wasn't appropriate for an airport waiting lounge. It just barely contained her full breasts and revealed more of her well-rounded ass than it hid. That dress would have worked fine in one of the island's beach bars, but not here, not in the semi-formal stiffness of the first-class lounge.

And those shoes! She had worn expensive fuck-me heels that had been removed and were now at her side. I imagined her long legs mounted on those platforms - yum. This was definitely a rich man's sex-toy... but why advertise it, I thought. Why, for instance, did he need to spread her knees? A demure knees-together position would have been much more effective - a modest counterpoint to her natural sexuality.

I could see a black thong between her legs. I did have to admit I thought this was sexy, especially the way it slipped into her crack, creating a pair of, well... lips. I looked at her mouth, then back to her cunt, then back again to her mouth, and smiled. Both pairs of lips were exceptionally round and full. Just right for warming somebody's cock at both ends, I thought rudely.

Maybe someday I'll buy my own CELT. I wonder what it would be like to own someone? This was just a dream of course - people like me didn't traffic in women; we didn't have anything to do with the CELT business. Not only that, I didn't have the personality for it. As much as I denied it, even to myself, I wasn't comfortable around girls. That's just the way it was, I thought sadly.

But I could still dream... I could feel myself getting hard as I studied her. People said that this was the problem with CELTs; they brought out the worst in men.

Not that this aspect of contract-girls bothered many people anymore. Consensual bondage was practically an institution now and CELT contracts were common. Didn't I just read that 5 percent of the women in the U.S. under thirty were CELTs? Legalization made sense, I thought, with today's overpopulation. People needed a way out of their poverty. After a few years a CELT, which stood for Contracted Escort Long Term, could earn enough money to make a new life for themselves, and often for their entire family. This made sense to a lot of people, despite the moral issues.

Of course, only a tiny fraction of the world's billions, just the most beautiful, the healthiest, the smartest made it out this way. Natural selection, I thought. Maybe this was why there was so much prejudice against CELTs?

But still, even with a CELT good taste was important. Just sitting there, his girl was giving half the room a hard-on. That wasn't right. Most sensible people tried to avoid trouble by downplaying the sexual aspect of CELT ownership. This girl's attire and her bondage were much too risqué for the lounge - more appropriate for a private men's club or a bondage bar, I thought prissily.

Nowadays it wasn't that unusual to see CELTs bound, even hard-bound, in public. Although it was still shocking to some, it was fairly common in Manhattan, for example, to see a girl being walked on a leash with her arms bound. It was chic, fashionable.

This girl's owner seemed to be trying for that look. He had tied her wrists and elbows together behind her back with narrow strips of soft white leather. Another strap had been wrapped twice around her neck, almost like a fashionable choker. The leather was so supple that the ends were simply tucked in, giving her that perfect no-knot look. I wondered if this leather tightened when it dried, like rawhide; that would be something to watch on this one, I thought evilly.

Despite the inappropriateness of it all, I grudgingly acknowledged that she looked incredible in her bondage - every man's fantasy slave-girl. As I said, it was just... too much. Her sexy bindings were supposed to create an illusion, I thought. The choker, for example, was making her pant like a dog and the elbow tie was pulling her shoulders back much too far. This wasn't pain for fashion's sake, it was torture.

Was I being too critical? The girl did look valuable - something you would see in a French fashion magazine. She also looked a little dangerous with that sleek, muscled body. Maybe the unusually harsh bondage and all that bare skin were intended to create an altogether different look - punishment for her haughtiness? Whatever, she was certainly stimulating a lot of fantasies.

Unconsciously my mind started to drift. I imagined her with me in my shower. She was on her knees, wrists tied behind, looking up at me with frightened glances as I deep-fucked her soft mouth. Her luscious full lips gripped my cock hard and I could feel her throat muscles moving rhythmically, swallowing to take me more fully inside. In my dream I reached down and pushed her away. She moaned in protest.

I shifted in my seat and surreptitiously repositioned my cock.

Back in the shower the girl looked up at me confused, her mouth and tongue still moving, memory-fucking my cock. Fighting the urge to reinsert myself, I reached behind her and lifted her bound wrists. She scrambled to her feet, bending forward at the waist. I hooked a chain hanging from the shower's ceiling to her wrists and then expertly tied her forearms together.

I ran my hands along her back and flanks as I moved to her rear. She was up on her toes, the ridges of her leg muscles sharply outlined. I watched her struggle. The mound between her legs darkened as it filled with aroused blood.

I moved in from behind, pushing my cock lengthwise between her pussy lips. I didn't want to enter her just yet. By instinct she inched forward on her toes until she was over my cock, and then she pushed herself down. I heard her moan from the new pain in her arms. Cruelly I laughed and started to pull out. Her cunt tightened. It was a delicious sensation, but I had another hole in mind this morning.

Squirting shampoo into her ass, I pointed my cock and pushed. She cried out, squirming. But the pressure was unrelenting and slowly I worked my way inside. In a few seconds she was fully impaled. Laughing again I grabbed a leather paddle hanging nearby and spanked her wet flanks. Immediately her squirming settled into a steady rocking motion - a gait. I enjoyed this for a time and then gave her a single sharp whack. She responded immediately, increasing her fucking speed to a slow trot. I waited a bit and then did it again and again. Each time she went a little faster. When she reached a full gallop I exploded inside, triggering her orgasm. Quickly I shifted my hands to her stomach to enjoy the contractions of her rock-hard abs.

Glancing around the lounge I shook off the daydream. Even though no one had seen it, I was embarrassed. My cock was like a piece of wood and I thought about going to the men's room to jerk-off. No, I thought, someone might walk in on me, but there was no going back to my computer now.

Instead I resumed my furtive examination, focusing on the outline of her bullet-like nipples pushing through the dress. I didn't think they were artificial; she just looked too young and fresh. But was anyone really born with such perfect nipples? What would it be like to grind them between my teeth...? Stop it, not again!

This was all just too much, I thought. No wonder I'm sitting here getting off. This outrageous display was pushing me beyond my limits. I could tell from their shifting eyes that the others in the lounge, mostly vacationers and a few businessmen, had the same feelings.

In fact the only person looking directly at the CELT was a plain-looking newlywed a few seats away, and her gaze was pure hatred. It seemed her new husband, a mousey man who was now studying his golfing magazine with way too much intensity, had been caught looking. I wondered what his married life was going to be like.

I shrunk down a little lower behind my laptop. Where did such a perverse dream come from? There should be limits, I thought, even for a fantasy. It wasn't exactly my fault, though. The man who owned this girl was the culprit! In another airport in another country someone in authority would have already spoken to him about their decency rules and about public punishment of CELTs. But this was the Caribbean. Things were done differently around here. Most of the time officials acted only when someone complained.

Maybe the plain girl will say something, I thought. Then again, why would she? She was probably enjoying the girl's suffering, which now appeared to be quite intense. Her neck strap was way too tight. Yes, she was definitely in trouble. I glanced around. Maybe some bystander would intervene? Unlikely; the CELT's owner was an aggressive lout. This was obvious from the heated argument he was having at the counter with a petite but determined ticket agent; something about a seat. Getting involved would probably result in an ugly confrontation, and for what? Technically the man wasn't doing anything wrong. She was just a CELT.

Not only that, this was a public place. If she was in real trouble all she needed to do was ask for help, just give us a sign. Someone would help her. But uninvited, no; people in crowds just didn't act that way. No one wanted to interfere, to look foolish. And certainly not me; I'd spent my entire life hanging back to avoid public mistakes.

This was really unusual, though, I thought again. Despite her apparent distress she wasn't making a sound. Normally a contract-girl would be whimpering like a puppy by now. One of the people nearby would then warn the man in the same way someone would tell him that something was leaking from his luggage. Not a criticism, just one traveler helping out another.

As I watched I could see that she was actively resisting. She just wasn't going to ask for help. Strange; typically the last thing a CELT wanted was to attract negative attention, especially from strangers. They prized their lucrative contracts and went to great lengths to avoid even the hint of a serious problem. Problems might lead to a formal complaint, maybe even a legal action, maybe even contract nullification. This was extremely rare, of course, but the threat was real. I was glad I had decided to stay out of it.

I'm a respectable banker, for heaven's sake, I told myself, here on business. How would it look if I actually got mixed up in something like this? I hadn't even gone to the beach on this trip, although I had secretly watched the women and the hard-bound, half-naked CELTs from my balcony.

Maybe one day I could afford a discretely hidden-away contract-girl of my own...

Our eyes met! She was staring at me. She was begging for my help, my personal help! I panicked and for a second I couldn't think. It was as if someone had touched me with a live wire. Maybe I should notify the desk? Then again, she wasn't really asking for help, not in the right way. She was supposed to whimper, whine; maybe cry a little. This would allow someone to report her distress in the right way. What could I possibly say? 'Ah, excuse me, Sir, I'd like to talk to you about the way you're treating your CELT.' I'd look ridiculous. CELTs don't just flash their eyes at someone and make him their champion. Not only that, it would embarrass and insult her owner, and no matter how big a jerk he was...

Anyway, the rules were different for her. It wasn't as if a normal person was in trouble. Legally she wasn't much more than a pet. So what if she suffered a little. I broke eye contact and stared down at the keyboard. Maybe she would get someone else's attention if I ignored her. I really didn't want to get involved in this. I started to work feverishly on my spreadsheet. I had no idea of what I was typing. I just didn't want to get involved.

I typed gibberish for almost a minute, then I looked up. She was still watching me as she worked to suck air into her lungs, but no longer pleading with her eyes. Clearly she had given up on me as her champion. I felt relief, then without warning she started to swoon. I could see her struggling desperately to take in more air. After a few seconds her color returned. There was perspiration on her upper lip. She looked at me defiantly with her nostrils flared. Then she turned away.

This was totally ridiculous. What could I do? Let the bitch suffer! This fucking CELT had too much pride for her own good. She was bringing this trouble on herself. I could feel myself getting angry. How dare she drag me, a total stranger, into her problem?

No, it was definitely better to just stay out of this. I resumed my nonsense typing. In the back of my mind, however, I could hear a small voice repeating one word softly over and over - coward - and deep inside I knew it was true.

CHAPTER TWO

The man returned from the counter and sat down on the lounge seat next to the girl. He was angry, shoving his ticket roughly into a paper folder. I could see from the color of the folder that he was in first class, same as me.

'Fucking airline,' he muttered to no one in particular. I could tell he was fuming. Then he looked at the girl and a smile seemed to cross his face. Without a word he sat forward on the edge of the seat and moved his leg to screen the girl a little. Reaching into his jacket pocked he extracted two round metal objects that looked like thick metal washers. Careful not to let him see me looking, I studied them; they had sharp triangular points on the inside rim and push-tabs on the outer edges. Discretely he pulled down the girl's dress, squeezed the tabs, and pinched one over a bare nipple.

I was horrified. Her entire body stiffened and her bare feet curled into claws. The first shock of pain lasted only a few seconds, but to me it seemed to go on forever. Amazingly she still didn't make a sound. Then he did the same to the other nipple with much the same effect.

Numb, I thought about what I had seen. Those 'washers' were brutal nipple clamps. The pain must be excruciating.

The man settled back in his chair, pleased with himself. It was as if the girl's pain had absorbed his anger. He seemed unconcerned that his vicious act of pique would be noticed by anyone.

I watched her out of the corner of my eye, still pretending to be focused on my spreadsheet. A sheen of sweat now covered her body and a tear meandered down from each tightly closed eye. Appalled and still feeling ashamed, I hid my face behind my screen.

'Hey, pal,' he called to me across the aisle. 'Would you mind watching my stuff while I go to the John?' He pointed with his thumb to his bags and the girl.

I looked up, trying to look innocent. 'Sure, sure no problem,' I said, much too quickly.

'Thanks,' he said, smiling. 'Want me to grab you a cup of coffee on my way back?'

'No thank you,' I said, with the barest hint of a judgmental tone.

He looked me over as he stood up. Then with a bit of irritation he said, 'Don't let anyone touch the girl, okay?' His meaning was clear; *and keep your fucking hands off her as well*. Then he seemed to think for a moment and turned back to her to remove her neck strap.

Glancing down to my lap as he passed, he smiled and gave a knowing nod. Embarrassed, I realized that the computer had slipped down and the bulge in my pants was showing. I readjusted the computer and once again starred at the keyboard as if searching for a missing letter.

I should have said something to him, I thought, as he walked away, but who was I to criticize this stranger? She was his legal property. It might not be very polite or appropriate to hurt her in an airport lounge, but he certainly had the right... nothing to get very upset about. Was I trying to provoke a confrontation? Again I had the sickening thought of trying to explain my involvement to the people at work.

When I finally looked up the girl was staring at me again, the two tears drying on her flushed cheeks. 'Don't let him rattle you,' she said softly. 'That's what he does for a living - shakes people up enough so they make mistakes. I'm sorry I bothered you before. Please don't tell him.' She seemed frightened; apparently he was capable of a lot worse.

'No problem,' I said, trying to sound casual. 'Do they hurt?' Idiot! *Do they hurt?* What a stupid question.

She nodded. 'He uses them a lot...' She paused as another wave of pain passed over her face. This explained the shape of the girl's nipples, I thought insensitively. Frequent use of the clamps had trained them into hard points.

I was totally unnerved, and before I could stop myself another stupid question passed through my lips. 'Why are you with him?' I was appalled; it was a totally absurd and inappropriate thing to ask. Her face froze and she was silent. Why was I being so incredibly dumb? In the back of my mind I realized I was trying to defend myself in her eyes. It was stupid. She was just a CELT; who cared what she thought?

She remained silent, and despite my rationalization I felt terrible. One didn't apologize to a CELT, but maybe in this case... Fortunately she raised her eyes and started to speak softly again, before I could put my foot back into my mouth.

'I didn't contract directly with him, Sir. My obligation was transferred.' She looked defensive. 'My family needed the extra money; my brother was sick.'

I was surprised; not at her sob story, everyone had one of those, but that she had a transferable contract. Almost all CELT contracts were non-transferable. A transferable contract meant you might end up with a very nasty stranger, like this one. Three years of legal bondage, the typical contract period, could feel like thirty in the wrong hands. Not only that, but transferable contracts were much more difficult to reverse. The courts had ruled a number of times that the consenting adults signing such contracts generally accepted greater risks, and that bad treatment by itself did not constitute grounds for reversal. I had been interested in this subject and studied the Consensual Bondage Laws of the 2120s quite extensively while in business school.

Still acting the idiot, and probably still trying to salvage my pride, I pursed my lips and shook my head. Then, with a critical air, my eyes shifted to the outline of the nipple clamps visible through her dress. The meaning was clear - this is what happens to silly girls who engage in such foolish behavior.

She looked at me for a moment, and then bent her head in silence. We had both said too much. In a few moments the man returned.

The first boarding call was announced. The man reached over and removed her bindings. He left the nipple clamps on under her dress and she made no attempt to touch them. She was well trained, I thought. 'Let's go,' he said. She got to her feet stiffly and slipped on her sexy heels. Her legs were as magnificent as I had thought. Then bending down as modestly as she could, she picked up a leather bag and followed him to the ramp, never looking in my direction.

I was the last person in the lounge to board the plane - too embarrassed and ashamed of myself to take the chance of accidentally bumping into either of them again.

CHAPTER THREE

Shit! What miserable luck. The man was in the seat next to mine. I checked my ticket again - 6E. I tried to slip into my seat without being noticed.

'How you doing, partner?' he said in a friendly way. The girl was on the floor at his feet. She was hugging her legs, her wrists tied to her ankles. 'Sorry about this,' he said, pointing at her with his thumb. 'I tried to buy her a seat, but the plane's full. He glanced around the full first-class cabin to illustrate the point. We'll be a little tight, but I'll keep her on my side.'

'No problem,' I replied. 'There's plenty of room in these seats. I'll probably just work. You can let her move around a little if you want.'

He smiled. 'Thanks, later.' Then he went back to his magazine.

In a few minutes the stewardess walked by and stopped at our row. 'Can I get either of you something to drink?' she asked.

'Nothing for me,' I said.

'I'll have a beer, little lady,' the man said.

'Certainly,' she beamed falsely, and then she noticed the CELT. 'I'm sorry, Sir, she's going to need to be checked. We have some very nice cages in the hold specifically designed for contract-girls. I can gate-check her right here for you.' She started to reach into her apron pocket for a check slip.

'Hold on, little lady,' he snapped. 'This here's a pretty valuable piece of property. I'd rather just keep her with me.'

'Sir,' the false smile was cracking, 'it's regulations. You can't keep anything in the aisle. Everything, including this... woman... must fit in the overhead or go under your seat. Otherwise it's got to be checked. This one looks too tall to go under the seat.'

Airlines now allowed first-class passengers to transport their CELTs in first class, but this accommodation was really only for petite girls. Some men liked their CELTs small and tight, believing they were easier to handle and that the sex was better.

'She'll fit,' he said, showing his own annoyance now. 'Maybe you can get me one of those CELT-belts.'

'I'll get you a belt, Sir, but if she doesn't fit fully under the seat I'll need to insist that she be checked.' She wanted to get the last word.

In a few seconds she returned with a long wide belt and handed it to him, along with his drink. No words were exchanged.

'Frigid bitch,' he mumbled. 'Would you mind holding this, partner?' He handed me his drink, then positioned the girl between his feet and wrapped the belt around her legs and pulled back hard. The air rushed from her lungs. Then he tightened the belt a little more and buckled it. I could see it digging into her skin.

He reached into his seatback pocket, breathing a little heavily from the exertion. 'This bitch is one fucking pain in the ass,' he said as he unfolded a leather hood and placed it over her head, tightening its built-in collar around her throat. Then he pressed the girl down and pushed her headfirst under the seat in front with his feet. Her short dress rode up, but he didn't bother to pull it down.

'Nice, huh?' he said, pointing at her ass with his toe.

'Can she breathe in that thing?' I asked, forcing myself to speak casually.

8

'No, she's just gonna have to hold her breath for a while,' he chuckled. Then he took his beer from me, downed it in one greedy gulp, fluffed up his pillow and turned away.

I watched her toes curl and uncurl as she settled into her confinement. It was clear that she could breathe through the hood, but it wouldn't be pleasant or easy. It must also be getting really hot in there, I thought. After a while I looked away and sat back in my seat for the takeoff. This was none of my business, I thought again. Stay out of it. She was just a CELT... a CELT with a transferable contract. That basically made her a prostitute.

The stewardess stopped by once to check. It was obvious from her frown that the girl wasn't really fully beneath the seat, but she chose to ignore the infraction rather than start another argument. I smiled at her for this small mercy.

The plane took off without further incident, and I spent the next hour staring at the girl's feet, wondering what it was like for her. The plane's interior had been darkened and most of the passengers were sleeping when the man finally stirred. Stretching, he turned on his overhead light, unfastened his seatbelt and pulled the girl out. He sat her upright on the floor and removed her hood. Her face and hair were sweaty. Carelessly he wiped her off with a couple of drink napkins and then set her back against the plane's bulkhead beneath the small oval window, still bound hand-to-foot.

'Excuse me, partner,' he said, 'I need to visit the boy's room.' I smiled and politely moved my legs aside to let him pass.

When he was gone I looked at the girl. She was still trying to recover from the hood.

'He's a character,' I said, trying to be casually friendly.

She looked at me and smiled politely, but said nothing.

'He seems to know all the tricks,' I persisted, not willing to be put off. She was silent. 'He seems to know all the tricks, right?' I repeated.

'He's a sadistic pig,' she cursed, and immediately looked up, worried, shocked at her loss of control.

For a moment neither of us said anything. Then she started talking again, too fast. 'Not that he's done anything wrong, Sir. Our contract, of course, gives him the right to treat me just about any way he wants. He's maybe a little too harsh. We just need more time to get used to each other.'

She thought for a moment and then resumed her desperate monologue. 'Please Sir, please, if you have one ounce of mercy in you please don't tell him what I said.' She was afraid, but it also appeared that beneath the surface she resented the need to beg for my help.

I thought about this for a minute. The responsible thing to do was to tell the man everything. If, God forbid, something bad happened in the future and it was discovered that I could have prevented it by warning him, I could be sued. An angry CELT is not a good thing to have sleeping in your bed, or even at the foot of it.

Still, was that necessary? It would get me further entangled with these two. Shit, why couldn't I have just kept my mouth shut? I thought for a moment and then I had what seemed to be a good idea. 'Maybe you should speak to him. Your contract gives you the right to protest, to contact your attorney. Why don't you try that?' I suggested.

She looked at me as if I were an idiot. 'Why should he talk to me? My contract has only a year to run. He knows I can't end it now. It would mean the loss of all further compensation.' Then her eyes filled. 'And that would mean the end of my family, the death of my brother.' She was getting worked up again, emotional; exactly what I was trying to avoid.

'Yes, I guess that is a problem,' I said dismissively. I didn't have an answer for her and, more importantly, I didn't want to get into a heavy discussion with a CELT whore. She was nothing to me. Why was I even bothering to talk to her; it was stupid. She had created her own problem; complaining about it afterward made her what, a cheat?

She glared at me and suddenly I was glad she was tied. In a low voice she started talking again. 'Yes, it's a problem...' She wasn't hiding her anger now, and most of it was directed at me. How did I get into this mess?

'Let me tell you what he did to me last night.' She was whispering, but every word was sharp. 'He made me strip down to a thong he likes, tied my arms behind my back, and locked my ankles together with a short hobble-chain. He likes to watch me run.' Her voice dropped even lower. 'Then he put his piranhas on me. That's what they're called, piranhas. I know you saw them earlier. It's like being eaten alive.'

She paused for a second to regain some composure. 'He attached a Y-leash and walked me around the hotel, stopping at every party to check out the action. Can you imagine what its like to be displayed naked on a leash... with other women watching? At one party he put me on my knees then tied the leash to a coat rack and hooked the hobble-chain to my wrists. I had to balance myself with my nipples. Everyone thought it was hilarious. Maybe you should try that with your cock, computer-boy, before you criticize me. They make piranhas for men, you know.' She stopped and started to cry. They were silent tears, and the way she wiped them away on her knees reminded me of a little girl.

'Look, I'm sorry,' I said in a whisper. 'I didn't mean to put you down before; it's just that this is none of my business. It's also not right for you to talk that way about your contract owner. As you said, he can do whatever he wants with you. In fact, if I don't tell him about this conversation and something happens I could be sued.'

She wiped away her tears again and looked at me with absolute loathing. 'Go ahead, tell him,' she spat out. 'Maybe he'll punish me right here and the two of you can get off. A cowboy-sadist and a Wall Street-coward; you two could be great friends.' She stared at me defiantly, and we both jumped when the man reappeared in the aisle.

He was carrying a glass of ice and four small bottles of vodka. 'I raided the liquor closet,' he said jovially, ignoring the tension that was hanging between us. 'She's a good looker, no? He glanced at me as he moved sideways back into his seat.

'Yes,' I said, red-faced, 'very nice.' I started to reach for my computer, trying to avoid any more conversation. The flight was turning into a nightmare.

But now the man was fully awake and talkative. 'Won her a few weeks ago in a card game,' he said in a conspiratorial whisper as he poured his first drink. 'Fella was drawing to an inside straight. He was so happy to make it that he thought he owned the pot and bet the farm, including her. Bad way to play! I had a full house from the get-go. He never knew what hit him. Been fucking her every night since. Amazing muscles, good moves... I just needed to teach her some manners. Now she's okay. Amazing things they got these days to keep these CELT bitches in line.'

I thought about the piranhas.

'Yup... I got an electric whip in my bag I've used on her a couple of times. It hurts like hell, but it don't make any marks. Copper's woven right into the leather braid.

You don't need to kill yourself, even a light stroke gets her full attention.' Glancing over to be sure I was listening, he continued. 'Best thing is to put them up by their wrists and get them on their toes. Then put a good gag on 'em and you're in for some real fun. Jesse here is strong and defiant. She'll kick for half-an-hour - maybe 20 strokes with the electric whip.' He paused and took a sip of his drink. 'Can't go too fast with the power turned up, you know; they'll pass out on you. Got to give 'em time to rest.'

He lowered his voice and moved a little closer. 'You also want her conscious when you're finished. That's the best time to fuck 'em, you know, right after, when their brain's still sparkin'. Give you a real ride.' He laughed and, not knowing what else to do, I smiled and nodded my head in agreement.

The girl looked up at me. I knew what she was thinking. This made me a little angry. No one, not even me, likes to be called a coward, especially by a stranger... a CELT. This bitch was purposely antagonizing me and impulsively I asked him, 'What do you do when she complains about you... to other people?' The girl's face turned white.

He glanced at Jesse, then said, 'Naw... Jesse wouldn't do that. She knows I won't put up with that kind of foolishness. If she did that to me I'd whip her hard for days. I know exactly how much she can take; I could easily keep her screaming for a week.'

He looked at me intently. 'She didn't bother you with any tall tales while I was in the John, did she, partner?' he asked. I knew he was watching to see if I glanced at the girl.

'No. No, she didn't say anything to me,' I lied. 'I was just wondering.' I never blinked or took my eyes off his.

'That's good, real good,' he said slowly. His jovial mood returned and he paused to sip his drink. Then he looked at her again. 'Got to keep that whip oiled up, right Jess? Don't want the leather to stiffen up.' Then he turned back to me. 'The best thing for a whip is the oil from a girl's skin. I know you think I'm shittin' you, but it's true. Just keep turnin' the whip to make sure it covers every part.' He casually sipped more of his iced drink.

'Probably sell her contract when I get back,' he continued. 'She's too much trouble, too much baggage for my line of work. There are plenty of girls around to rent. No need to carry my own around with me. Am I right?'

'What line of work is that,' I asked, ignoring his question and trying desperately to sound friendly. I was thinking about the pain my vicious little remark might cause her.

'Well, I'm pretty much retired now, but I do some gambling from time to time. Keeps life interesting, you know. You ever play?' It sounded like a question he had asked many times before.

'No, not really,' I said. 'Well, sometimes, just for fun.'

'Tell you what,' he leaned even closer, 'how would you like to play for this here girl? I've seen you eying her. She'd make a great bed-warmer. And like I said, she's strong and tough... takes a lot of pain.'

I looked at him, knowing he was joking, putting me on. 'What's she worth?' I asked, playing along.

'About a hundred grand now, still got another year or so to run on her contract.' He was bragging, showing off.

I nodded my head, smiling, still going along with the wind up. Then my mouth opened and I heard myself saying, 'Okay, I'll bet you a hundred thousand dollars, against her contract. One cut of the cards.'

I couldn't believe my ears! What was I doing? In a panic I realized that a quick laugh would make the statement sound like a joke. I needed to laugh! Laugh, you fool!

But something held me back. It was the only truly brave thing I had ever done.

The girl looked at me, openly curious, possibly even hopeful. The man's eyes narrowed and he shoved his face close to mine. 'I was just kidding, partner.' Then he leaned back in his seat and was quiet for a few minutes, sipping his drink pensively.

Then slowly he turned to me, and asked, 'You got a hundred thousand dollars... *partner?*'

'Yes,' I said simply, holding his gaze. Actually I had $108,000 - my life's savings. WHAT WAS I DOING?

The man looked at me for a long moment. I held my breath. Maybe he would laugh the whole thing off. Then he glanced at the girl. Guilt was written all over her face, and he knew immediately that we had talked, and that most of that talk had been about him. I could see him turn a little red with anger.

He nodded and looked back at me. Then he smiled. The girl was going to be whipped exactly as he had described. A personal insult was an important thing for him. She realized it at the same time and trembled. She clearly knew the difference between casual pain and real punishment.

But now he wanted something from me as well. I had apparently violated some unwritten gambler's code. 'OK, pal, you come up with the dough and it's a bet.' His tone was no longer friendly, it was distinctly hostile.

I hid my fear. Maybe I could just laugh now, roll over and go to sleep. Who cares what this creep thinks or says? So he punishes her... so what? The truth is that she deserves it. Well, maybe she doesn't deserve being whipped for a week, and maybe I was partially responsible for egging her on, but so what? She's just a CELT, remember!

Every logical part of my brain desperately wanted me to laugh it off and forget it - forget about her. But I just couldn't. Without thinking I reached into my wallet and retrieved my debit card. I swiped it through the seatback reader with a shaking hand. Using a few keystrokes on the seat's built-in computer I moved a hundred thousand dollars into an escrow account and assigned it a password, writing it secretly on a paper napkin. He watched all this with a smirk on his face.

'You sure seem to know what you're doing with that banking stuff,' he said. Then he stood up and pulled his large leather bag out of the overhead locker. Unzipping an outside pocket he found the girl's contract. I could see that it already had several transfer endorsements on the back.

'She sure is going to look good at your feet if you win,' he said. 'I'm also gonna throw in everything in this bag. You'll need it to keep her in line.' I could tell I was being worked now. He smelt my money. I was now his pigeon, or whatever gamblers call their prey.

'Thanks,' I said quietly, glancing at the girl. This was lunacy. I was about to lose my life's savings for an exotic pet - a whore.

'Well, okay!' he said emphatically, ringing the call button. In a few seconds the same stewardess appeared. 'Ma'am, would you mind getting my friend and me a pack of your best playing cards?' She nodded stiffly and went for them. We waited in silence.

When the cards arrived he shuffled them on the divider between our seats. His hands moved like a magician's. I was glad this was a simple cut of the deck.

'You know what,' he said, placing the deck between us, 'let's bring Jesse into this.' Reaching into his bag he pulled out the piranhas and dropped them into his jacket pocket. Then he extracted a ball gag. Moving the girl between his legs he pushed the gag into her mouth and tightened it behind her head. Reaching back into the bag he found a high leather collar, and I knew this was for discipline.

'What are you doing?' I asked.

'You can let her out when you win,' he said, tightening the collar around her throat.

'And if I lose?' I asked.

'Then you can watch her for the next three hours,' he snorted, buckling the collar so tightly her face turned red. She wasn't getting enough air.

'Look, there's no reason for this,' I said, starting to panic. The girl was barely able to breathe. A blunt point at the top of the collar kept her head high so that she was staring directly at me. I was reminded of the scene at the airport.

He was having sadistic fun with both of us and enjoying himself. He was also continuing to work me, ensuring that I had yet another reason to continue with the bet.

'Okay, I'll tell you what, partner,' he said reasonably. 'Once our bet is finished I'll let her out.' I knew it was a lie. Once he won we would both be at his mercy. Jesse would stay in the collar until she passed out, then he would devise some other torture for her. He wanted us to suffer and he knew that punishing her was painful to me as well. The girl looked at me with her mouth open, breathing hard. She was now working hard to survive. I smiled at her reassuringly, but I felt sick.

'Come on, kid,' he urged. 'Don't lose your balls now. This one's tough. She can take it, can you? Worry about yourself. It's your money.'

What a vicious bastard, I thought. I can't let him whip her for a week because of something I did.

'Okay,' I said defiantly. 'Let's get this over with.'

He smiled again and turned to the girl. 'You got yourself a real champion here, Jess. Man's willing to put up a hundred thousand dollars to keep your pretty ass from a little punishment.'

He was absolutely gleeful. 'My name's Max, by the way, Max Springer,' he said as he held out his hand. 'And this here is Jesse. I don't like to gamble with strangers.'

'I'm Howard Lowe,' I said, returning his handshake with a limp wrist. My face was ashen and despite my earlier resolve, I was afraid.

'Howard,' he repeated, turning the name around scornfully in his mouth. He was really enjoying himself. Then he pulled the piranhas out of his pocket and held them up for both of us to see. 'These little babies are amazing,' he said, squeezing the side tabs and demonstrating the pinching movement of the inside points. 'And the name really fits. They can really bite.'

He slipped Jesse's dress down to her waist. She sat on the floor half naked, bound and gagged. We both looked down at her from our plush seats. She stared back at us, unashamed. Grabbing one of her breasts Max held it tight as he squeezed the piranha over her nipple and slowly released the tabs. Jesse closed her eyes and absorbed the pain. I could see it was a lot worse now since her nipples were already sore. Max would have known that.

He watched her anguished face for a moment and then did the same to her other breast. Pulling her dress back up he muttered, 'We'll leave her covered. Don't want to upset the stewardess, now do we?'

He whispered to the girl loudly enough for me to hear. 'You'll be okay, Jesse. Just keep thinking about how much worse it will be when we get home. She held my eyes. I could see fear; this was no idle threat. The man really was a sadistic pig, just as she had said.

'I hate to see her cry,' he said, then smirked arrogantly, and that was when I lost my nerve.

'Let me ask you a question,' I said with a shaky voice. 'Suppose I just buy out her contract? You said you were thinking about selling it anyway, this way we both end up with what we want.' This wasn't true at all, I thought. All I wanted was my hundred thousand dollars safely back in my account and to be free of this mess.

He looked at me like the street fighter that he really was. 'That might have been okay before, kid, but then you and Jess here went and made this personal. Personal is no good. This girl is my property. You fucked with her head without my permission. Now she's goin' have to pay for her mistake - and yours too.'

His arrogance put some steel in my back. I looked him in the eye and even managed to exhibit a bit of bravado. 'Well then, all that's left to do is cut the cards.' It was all show; I was scared and I knew he was going to win.

Placing the cards down, he gestured with his hand for me to take my cut. I managed to nod in his direction - you first.

Smiling, he reached down and cut the deck - a Jack. He just smiled, leaned down, and showed the girl the card. Her eyes closed in fearful resignation and I thought she had fainted, but then her eyes opened again and she looked at me. It was the look of someone condemned. 'I'll charge up the whip's batteries as soon as we get home, Jess, so you can start your week right.' He was enjoying every moment.

Then he looked over at me. 'Your card, How-word.'

I ignored his jibe, but my hand was shaking so badly I had trouble cutting the deck. I didn't even look at the card I'd drawn, just faced it towards him. He looked down from my eyes to the card, smiled broadly, and leaned back in his seat, happy. I had lost!

I was devastated. Three years' savings gone in a second and a week of vindictive torture for a girl who had just asked me for a little help. Surprisingly the money didn't seem all that important anymore as I thought about Jesse's beautiful body writhing at the end of the asshole's whip.

Oh man, what had I done? I felt sick.

Numb, I checked the card in my hand to see how close I had come. It was the queen of hearts. The queen of... the *Queen!*

Max looked at me, unfazed. 'Looks like you won, kid. Congratulations.' He picked up the contract, wrote in my name as owner and signed it. Then he put it back in the bag and gestured for us to change seats. Once he was settled he casually rolled over and went back to sleep. Gamblers don't linger at a losing table.

I was dumbfounded and sat there for some time enjoying the relief that coursed through my body. Then I remembered the girl and moved to her aid. I swore to myself that she would never suffer in my hands.

Reaching down I removed her gag, and then as gently as I could I took off the piranhas and put them back in the bag. I tried not to touch her breasts, but it was unavoidable. She was crying softly. I wiped her face and untied her hands and ankles. Still crying a little she moved between my feet and rested her head on my lap. I could feel her arm inching forward to find a secure place between my legs. I stroked the damp hair from her perspiring brow, and then got instantly hard when I realised her mouth was so near my cock. She probably noticed, but I didn't care. We had won!

When we started to descend she turned around and positioned herself for the belt. I put it back on and gently moved her halfway under the seat. Of course, I didn't use the hood.

Max, who had slept for most of the trip, finally woke up as we were landing and watched us with his smirk undiminished. When the plane arrived at the gate he stood up and gave me a quick goodbye handshake. 'You are the man, Howard,' was all he said. Then he was gone.

At the time I thought it was just a Max-like dumb thing to say. Later I would regard those four words as precious wisdom... most precious wisdom.

CHAPTER FOUR

'May I change my clothes, Master?' she asked.

We were standing outside the arrival gate at JFK airport. With the sundress exposing her bare shoulders and long legs, she was getting lecherous stares from the male passersby. I was embarrassed. 'Look, ah... Jesse, please don't call me that; my name is Howard. And you don't need my permission to change your clothes. That life is over for you. I'm a decent person, I don't treat women badly.'

She looked at me with a strange expression. 'Thank you, Ma... thanks, Howard. There are some jeans and a top in the bag. Maybe I could wear them?'

'That would be fine,' I said, but she just stood there holding the bag. I was confused. 'Go ahead,' I urged.

She glanced at me shyly and said, 'I'm not permitted to open it.' It was ridiculous, but I guess once you've been whipped for something, you learn.

'Look, I said, you don't...' then I stopped, frustrated. This wasn't the place to have this conversation. Bending down I opened the bag and handed her the pair of jeans and a top. She walked off to the ladies' room.

In a few minutes she was back. I held my breath. She looked incredible. People were still staring at us... at her. She was movie-star gorgeous.

Quickly I steered us to a cab line and we jumped in. 'Twenty-Eight East 79th Street,' I said to the driver, then added, 'please.' He nodded and drove off. We sat in total silence for the entire trip, both of us overwhelmed by the events of the last few hours.

I live in a Manhattan townhouse. I turned on some lights and directed her to the library and the wooden chair in front of my desk. I settled in my chair behind the desk.

'Let me explain a few things to you, Jesse,' I started as austerely as I could, trying to be very businesslike. 'I'm not rich. This is my grandfather's house; it's owned by a family trust. I have the right to use it, but not to sell or rent it. I also have a small trust that pays me a little allowance each month. That's all my grandfather left me. In other words, I'm not rich.' I paused and let her absorb what I'd just said. 'Do you understand?' I didn't want her to think I was... a mark.

She nodded.

'I live here alone, by choice,' I continued. Actually, the choice part wasn't really true. 'I don't socialize much... too busy at work.' This was getting too personal. 'I just don't have that many relationships,' I said, stupidly ending my clumsy explanation of why a 25-year-old, solvent, Manhattan-townhouse-residing man was living alone in Manhattan.

She nodded again while she looked around the room, and then asked the obvious question. 'Are you gay?'

'No,' I replied, and hurried on. 'You can stay here while we take care of the legal work. There are plenty of spare bedrooms. Tomorrow I'll call my lawyer and get him started on your emancipation.'

'Emancipation?' she asked.

'Yes, emancipation. There's no way I can hold on to your contract. I work in a bank, a vice president. It wouldn't look right. Not that I wouldn't want to be... associated... with you, any man would, you're beautiful. It's just that in my position, with my family, it would just be, well inappropriate. Even though what happened tonight was all innocent, it would be just too hard to explain. Don't worry; I'll make sure you get paid the full amount agreed to in the contract.'

She was quiet for a moment. 'I'm sorry about what I said before on the plane, Master... um, Howard.' She was looking down. 'The pain was getting to me. Thank you for your help in working things out with Mr Springer. I know it's inappropriate to say such things, but he was an animal. It was a brave and generous thing to do.'

We both knew that this little speech was bullshit - for the most part I had let her down time after time - but it was easier for us to accept the picture the way she had just painted it. If I had just left it there things would have worked out very differently, but instead my mouth began again.

'I'm not sure how long the legal work will take, but if you're okay with it we can just pretend that you're my live-in girlfriend for a few days. This way, when you leave, I can just say we broke up. As I said, I haven't had much time for girls, but people will accept this explanation. The last thing I want is for anyone to know that I owned a CELT contract. Even though I didn't do anything wrong, I don't want to have to explain this, ever.' I paused again.

'Or if you'd rather stay at a hotel I can make a few calls. You won't need to worry about the expenses; I'll pay for everything. In either case I'll treat you with the utmost respect and, of course, there won't be any physical abuse. I find that reprehensible. Hopefully Max is the last man who will ever... Anyway, for all practical purpose we can consider your CELT contract ended right now. You are my guest.'

I smiled in what must have looked like a self-righteous way and sat back in the chair. She looked at me with a strange expression, and in a matter-of-fact tone said, 'Won't we need to fuck, Howard, if we're going to be boyfriend and girlfriend?' Was there a hint of sarcasm in her voice?

Her directness surprised me, and I needed a moment to recover.

'No, we don't need to do that, Jesse,' I said slowly, thinking that she may be relating to this kind of decent treatment after what she'd been through. I also had the idea that she might not be that bright. 'We're only going to act like lovers, but in truth we'll just be employer and employee. You're an escort, remember? Someone people hire because they don't want to go places alone.' We both knew that was also bullshit; CELT escorts were sex-partners.

'Do you understand what I've told you?' It was almost the tone one would use with a child.

'Yes, I understand, Howard,' she began with equal patience. 'It's just that people always seem to know when a couple is fucking... someone might suspect something. Maybe you should think about it; fucking me might actually be the safest thing, reputation-wise.' She was copying my parent-child tone; she also sounded a little angry. Why?

'And when you say "no physical abuse",' she continued, 'you mean unless I deserve it, right? It wouldn't make sense for you to allow me to go without any discipline. Didn't you and Max agree that the best way to handle one of us was to, and I quote, "put them up by their wrists and get them on their toes... shove in a good gag and you're in for some real fun. This one will kick and jerk for half-an-hour...". You seemed to be listening very hard. Oh, and I almost forgot his most important suggestion, "fuck her while her brain is still sparking". Isn't that what you and he agreed?' She was definitely angry now. This was not going at all the way I expected.

'Look, Jesse, I don't think you understand...' I started again.

'And by the way, Howard,' she interrupted, 'I fast-tracked my way through high-school and college, graduating from NYU at twenty with a bachelor's degree in psychology. So don't keep asking me if I understand you. I said my family was in trouble, I didn't say I'd been poor and dumb all my life.

'Let's be honest with each other,' she continued. 'You didn't have the nerve to help me when I needed you, but now I'm supposed to believe that you're going to do the right thing for the sake of your reputation... your family; you're going to throw away a hundred thousand bucks.

'And what makes you think I want to be emancipated?' she asked. 'Don't you think the next man who buys my contract is going to wonder why I was set free early? Are you going to give him an affidavit attesting to your goodwill? CELTs are worth a lot, people don't just give one away without good reason.

'You didn't act out of honor or sympathy, Howard; you were distracted by that bulge in your pants and acted impulsively. It's that simple. Once you'd backed yourself into a corner you just followed the path of least resistance. It was all an accident that worked out okay for you. Once you have had some time to think it over, you'll come to your senses about me.' She was calming down.

'It's not that I don't appreciate what you did, Howard. Some of it truly was brave and Max really was a pig.' She paused and looked at me.

'Take my advice,' she leaned forward as if to emphasize her next words. 'Tie me up and hurt me a little over the next few days... just so you can see what it's like. I'm sure you'll like it. If you want you can fuck me as well or I can suck your cock. Then, when you've had your fill, sell my contract. That's what most men in your position would do. Believe me, I know. You won yourself a contract-girl worth a hundred thousand dollars tonight, Howard, enjoy her. As for the contract itself, I agree that it would be impossible for you to hold on to it, someone of your standing, but don't give it away.'

She leaned back and smiled at me with a now-doesn't-this-make-sense expression. But I was hurt. I guess I had started to think of 'us' as a team. She was right to set things straight. I would never hurt her, of course, and there was no way that I would force her to do anything sexual, but she was right about the money. Holy shit, in the last few hours I had doubled my net worth. Tripled it really if you adjusted for the taxes I didn't need to pay. I was also extremely tired. 'I'm not exactly sure why I did any of the things I did tonight, Jesse, but I'm not the kind of man who would take advantage of such a situation. Let me take you to your room.' I said this last with finality. 'We'll straighten it all out tomorrow.'

I left the house the next morning early, before she was awake. I wrote her a brief note saying she should make herself at home, and that if she wanted we could go to dinner that evening and talk. I also left her some cash to do some shopping, as she didn't seem to have many clothes.

I put the evening's discussion to the back of my mind. She had been tired and stressed. I should have waited to talk to her. She seemed like a decent person in a bad situation. We would get it all worked out tonight. In the meantime I'd get things started by talking to my lawyer about her contract. Once she really understood the kind of person I was it would be easier for us to talk.

The office was in chaos over something or other and I was in meetings for the entire day. It was a blessing in a way to be distracted from the 'Jesse problem'. But unfortunately I didn't get a chance to calling my lawyer.

CHAPTER FIVE

That evening when I got home she met me at the door dressed in black pants and a white silk top. The pants hugged her behind, highlighting her long legs. The outfit included a short jacket that accentuated her small waist. She was a classy dream... a Park Avenue debutant... no one would ever guess she was a CELT.

'Is this okay, Howard?' she asked innocently.

'It's perfect,' I replied enthusiastically. My relief was enormous. I wanted to kiss her and more, but held back. We hardly knew each other.

She waited and then leaned over and kissed me on the cheek. 'Thank you, again,' she said. Then she began to describe her day as we walked to my bedroom. She was effervescent, bubbling over with enthusiasm, talking lightly all the way to my door, where she waited modestly while I got dressed.

Being in New York City with time and money was an exciting experience, especially for a stunningly beautiful young girl. I knew she would have been propositioned at least half-a-dozen times that day. In fact, a part of me thought she might be gone when I got home, contract or not.

For the next hour we talked continuously without saying anything important. I forgot she was a professional escort, and despite my clumsiness around women, I felt a real rapport growing between us. She made everything easy and fun and there was no mention of yesterday's events or the prior evening's discussion. It was as if we were old friends.

We went out for dinner, which was even better. We talked about everything and nothing; it was a real date. It turned out that she was twenty-two, three years younger than me. Her family was from California with Russian roots. She had originally come to New York to get the East Coast educational experience. It was fun to talk about the stuff we'd done in college, and to exchange opinions on just about everything. She was incredibly sharp and smart, much smarter than I had imagined. For the first time in a long time, I was having fun.

Later, over coffee, we discussed her situation. She was open and unembarrassed. After college she had been looking for a job when her father was accused of embezzlement. Between the legal fees and fines the family, which had been reasonably well off, lost almost everything. He went to prison for eight years. Two months later her brother was diagnosed with cancer. The treatments needed to keep him alive were costly. She tried everything, but the only way she could get enough money for him was to become a CELT. Even then the non-transferable contracts didn't pay enough, so she needed to agree to the more lucrative transfer clause. Such a contract had come easily with her looks.

The sad moments in our conversation were when she talked about her mother and brother, whom she'd not seen for two years. Apparently both had fought her decision to become a CELT, calling his illness God's will. When she refused to listen they broke all contact with her. Her money was now funneled to them through a charitable foundation which, on her strict orders, took full credit for it. There was no bitterness in the explanation. 'Just my bad luck,' she said, with a sad smile.

Stupidly I asked if she was happy as a CELT. She looked at me almost with pity, and then said, 'Some parts of it are okay, like now. Others are a nightmare. Most women, for example, look at me as if I were a used condom.' She looked around at the other diners.

'It doesn't help to think about things in terms of happy or sad, Howard. It doesn't work that way. I just try to get through each day, one at a time, and deal with what comes along. As I said, some are good, other days I would be very happy to die. Unfortunately that option isn't available to me - CELT contracts terminate on accidental death or suicide.' There was no self-pity in the explanation.

'That part of your life is over, really Jess, I mean it,' I reassured her. 'It's unbelievable to me that anyone could mistreat a beautiful and talented girl like you.' She just smiled and nodded. Then she asked me about my story.

It was boring by comparison, but she encouraged me to talk. I told her about my family, which was wealthy; my job, which had been arranged through family connections at the bank; and about my grandfather's Manhattan townhouse, which he had left for me, his fifth grandson, to use. I explained that even though I was 'from money' and might someday inherit something from my parents, I wasn't rich myself... just an ordinary working guy with a fabulous place to live and a small but regular trust-fund allowance. Encouraged, I talked even about the little things - private school in Boston, summers in Rhode Island, high-school football, tennis and my small triumph getting to the Northeast College League's semi-finals, and my few love affairs, all of which had ended unhappily.

She related to everything, laughing and sighing at just the right times. It was as if we were best friends catching up with each other's lives.

Then it was time for desert. 'I'll have a piece of blueberry pie,' she told the waiter.

'And I'll take the chocolate mousse,' I said.

'Did you take care of the contract today, Howard?' she asked in the same carefree tone she had used all evening.

'No, sorry, I didn't get around to it. The office was a madhouse today. I'll take care of it first thing in the morning,' I promised.

She smiled. 'Thanks for this evening. I'm sorry I was such a bitch last night. You've been wonderful.' Then her voice lowered to a whisper. 'And thanks as well to that wonderful queen of hearts. If it wasn't for her I'd be hanging from Max's rope right now, dancing to his whip.' This was the first time she had directly referred to that part of a CELT's life. I was amazed at how casually she could talk about such a horror.

'Let's not talk about that stuff, Jess. I hate to even think of you being hurt that way. Anyway, its history, no one is ever going to hurt you again,' I promised.

She nodded and smiled. 'You promise?' she said, reaching for my hand. 'Not even a little spanking?' She was obviously just teasing me, but the thought of it was stimulating. 'Maybe you can tie me up in the shower, Howard, and make me suck you.'

I was shocked, and not a little disturbed that she had guessed the kind of thing that was on my mind; the shower scene was one of my strongest sexual fantasies. But I answered with equal nonchalance, as if she were joking, 'Nope, nothing; as you will see I'm a perfect gentleman.'

'There are no perfect gentlemen, Howard,' she said carefully, 'only those too repressed or too scared to give free rein to their real feelings.' Then her voice lifted and she laughed, 'You seem a little repressed yourself, Howard. I'll bet you a kiss that I could turn you into a Max-like sadist in an hour.'

I laughed with her and replied, 'That's just about the last thing I want to be, but feel free.' I was still joking around, trying to get us back to a normal conversation. 'I hope Max has gotten over losing last night. I suspect you were his walking bankroll for his next game.'

She nodded, then our deserts arrived.

'Excuse me,' Jesse said pleasantly to the waiter. 'I ordered the apple pie.'

'No, Miss, I'm sure you ordered the blueberry, but I will be happy to bring you apple instead,' he said politely.

'No, I ordered the apple,' she insisted, her voice still pleasant.

'Well, maybe you did,' he said in a placating way, humoring her. 'In any case, I'll be happy to change it for you.'

I could see she was getting annoyed. 'I'll tell you what,' she said, 'since you want to be right so badly, let's just say that this pie is your tip.' She was talking loudly enough now so that people at the surrounding tables started turning their heads.

'Jesse,' I said, 'take it easy, it's not worth getting upset over.'

'Sorry, I just don't like people who can't admit a mistake.' She was perfectly cool, but determined. 'Like this asshole here.'

That was when the waiter made a fatal mistake. 'Look, Miss, maybe it will mean my tip, which I can't afford to lose, but you ordered the blueberry. I'm certain of it.' Now everyone was glancing over.

She looked at him for a moment and then seemed to collect herself. 'Yes, I guess it's possible that I said blueberry without thinking.' I was relieved and the small room seemed to breathe a collective sigh of relief; finally she was being reasonable. I hated scenes. 'Maybe you're right. I'm sorry. I like blueberry too; why don't you just leave it?'

The waiter gave a little bow and turned, and the next few seconds seemed to move in slow motion. Horrified, I watched as she dumped the pie into her hand, stood up, and smeared it over the back of his white jacket!

For half a second the room froze, then it was pandemonium. Everyone was shouting and moving at the same time. I managed to pull Jesse into the foyer to deal with the manager. It took every ounce of personal charm I had to get out of there without police action, and of course the two hundred dollars I passed the waiter for his cleaning bill and tip didn't hurt.

'Why did you do that?' I asked her angrily in the cab, confused at the sudden turn of events.

'I hate liars,' she replied with amazingly calm.

'And that's the way you show it - by going crazy in public?' I was incensed.

'That waiter was a liar, just like you!' She looked at me with eyes blazing. I was amazed at the transformation. Twenty minutes ago we were like two kids on a first date. 'You promised me you'd take care of my contract today, but "somehow" you just couldn't find the time. Like I told you, Howard, the men I know make lots of promises they just don't get around to, at least with CELTs. It's really amazing how many times it's happened. You are just another version of those same pricks.'

After a brief pause she continued with real venom. 'No I take that back, Howard. Most of them have not been as hypocritical... as cowardly.'

'Jess, I want you to be quiet now.' I was steaming and thinking about how this was sounding to the driver. 'I told you I would take care of it, and I will,' I said in a forced whisper. 'And look, I use that restaurant all the time. You embarrassed me in there; not only that, it was totally unnecessary.' I was pissed.

'And by the way, you did order the blueberry.'

She turned a bright red, turned her face away and stopped talking. I was happy to let things settle down. When we reached the house she jumped out and ran to the door, opening it with a key she could only have gotten from my desk. Realizing this I was even more furious. She had been through my private things!

This had to stop... right now!

I handed the driver a twenty dollar bill and waited for my change, mostly to give myself time to calm down. Then I followed her slowly into the house. The light was on in the library. I was thinking about my opinions: throw the crazy bitch out in the morning; take her to a hotel; call my lawyer; call the cops. This scene was definitely not my style, and she was definitely too emotional, too erratic, too volatile for my taste. I was a quiet introverted kind of guy; loud, aggressive people turned me off.

It was sad though, I thought. She was someone I could have enjoyed being with. Why did she go nuts all of a sudden?

I was prepared for more craziness, but the scene in front of me when I reached the library door was way beyond crazy. Jesse was squatting on the rug, naked from the waist down, pissing on the Oriental rug in front of my desk! Max's leather bag was nearby. I was dumbfounded, quick-frozen to the floor. Strangely, my first thought was that the bag had been moved.

'This is what I think of your promises, you little coward,' she sneered at me across the room. 'You're just another liar. And don't ever tell me to be quiet again; I'll say what I want.' She was in an insane rage, but now so was I. The CELT bitch was pissing on my grandfather's rug...

For the first time in my amazingly genteel life, I literally saw red. Enraged, I crossed the space between us in a second and pushed her hard to one side. She hit her head on the desk and was momentarily stunned. Seizing the advantage I sat astride her hips and pinned her arms in the small of her back. She recovered within seconds and started to scream. Not just scream; to buck, kick, bite - I had a wildcat on my hands.

Desperate to control her I frantically looked around the room. The only thing within reach was the bag. I pulled it to me. Inside, right on top, were the soft leather binding strips. Hadn't I pushed them to the bottom when I got her clothes? Whatever...

She was strong, but fortunately I was stronger and quickly had her wrists tied. Unbelievably she was still trying to kick me, so grabbing another strap I tied her ankles, bent her legs at the knees and lashed her wrists to her ankles. It wasn't painful, just restraining.

'Let me out of this you coward!' she screamed. 'You're a weakling and a liar!'

I was panting and shaken. This was scary stuff. Where was the wonderful girl I'd been with tonight? Where was the vulnerable girl who'd cried on my knee last night on the plane? I needed her to stop talking, right now.

Dumping the bag's contents on the floor I found a ball gag and pushed it against her closed lips. She refused to open them, and with a sudden shake of her head knocked it out of my hand.

'Don't start something you can't finish, little coward!' she raged. 'I've been tied by real men - men with balls. You think you can compete with them?'

Again I saw red, and in an insane moment of my own I grabbed her hair and pulled her head back. Then I roughly shoved the gag into her mouth, dropped her head and tightened the strap behind her neck. Still in a rage I spied the leather hood and pulled that over her head as well, fastening its collar around her neck.

Emotionally drained and exhausted, I sat back in a chair to calm myself. Jesse also quieted slowly. What an incredible mess. Did I really need to tie her up this way? Just until she calmed down, I told myself. She really could have hurt me, or herself. Maybe she needed psychiatric help. She must be bipolar or something; an hour ago we had been laughing, sharing personal experiences, even secrets.

When I was sure she had settled down I cautiously removed the hood. She looked at me normally, even a little embarrassed. I took out the gag.

'I'm sorry, Jesse, I thought you were going to hurt yourself.' I was embarrassed and started to move to untie her wrists.

'Don't worry about it, Howard,' she said in an absolutely calm and rational voice. 'People get carried away and abuse their CELTs all the time. We'll let our lawyers sort this out. I'll try to keep it out of the newspapers.'

I froze. What? Lawyers? Newspapers? I'd be fired. I returned to the chair and sat down, shaken.

'Let me out of this, Howard, or I'll call the cops first chance I get. How good do you think it's going to look to have flashing lights on your street? Every additional second I stay in this is another...'

I jumped up and roughly shoved the ball gag back into her mouth and replaced the hood. I couldn't handle any more graphic detail of exactly how my life was going to be flushed down the toilet.

I returned to my chair and watched her. Was this really as bad as she implied? I would need to explain what had happened, but people would understand. It wasn't as if I went to a CELT auction and bought myself a contract. My family also had some of the best lawyers around.

As I calmed myself I watched her. She certainly had great legs, and a great ass...

'Fuck this,' I said out loud, still angry, and retrieved a pair of scissors from my desk. I paused for a moment, watching her ass, then I used the scissors to cut off the rest of her clothing. She struggled violently and tried to say something through the gag. But did I really care what she had to say now? Not really. I was finished with her, so what difference did it make?

I returned to my chair once again. What a magnificent body. I took my time and examined every inch of it. I also paused to admire my hurried bondage. Without thinking about it I had crossed her ankles and wrists, splaying her knees and elbows to the sides and preventing her from rolling over. Not a bad job for a novice, I thought. She was completely restrained.

Is that all I wanted - to restrain her? Shouldn't she pay in some way for her outrageous behavior? Isn't that why CELT contracts allowed physical discipline? I examined my feelings. The rug she had pissed on was probably ruined. It had been worth a lot of money. The scene she created in the restaurant had embarrassed me in front of a lot of people. Not only that, but her insults and threats were clear challenges to my, albeit temporary, authority. Wasn't I entitled to the respect due an owner until she was emancipated? Fuck all that, wasn't I entitled to the respect due someone who had risked everything to help her?

The more I thought about it the more incensed I became. If any CELT ever deserved to be punished, it was her. I really would be a coward if I let all of this go by without responding in a way that was expected with a CELT. Was I really the coward she kept calling me?

I spent a few more minutes thinking, then I walked over and, using a long strap from Max's bag, I looped her wrists and ankles even tighter together, really putting a strain on them, and by lifting her legs while pulling on the strap I was able to arch her back until her body was pulled into a tight bow. I stopped when her knees were fully off the floor and all her weight was on her breasts. Then I tied a strap to the loop at the top of her hood and pulled her head back hard, tying it off to another strap I cinched around her elbows.

Her body whipsawed violently during the process, but each new tie restrained it a little more until the whipping motion turned into minor jerking. Hesitantly at first, I ran my hands over her breasts. They were incredible. Then for some reason I pinched her nipples. I could hear her grunting through the hood. I did it again, harder. Her body jerked violently in protest. I did it again, even harder. I could hear her protests turning into a cry of real pain - and I enjoyed it.

I stood back to admire my work. Her breasts and ass were rock hard under the strain of the bow; in fact all her muscles were straining to relieve the pressure on her back. Her knees were pulled apart, allowing me an unrestricted view of her cunt, which I noticed was glistening wet.

I returned to my chair to watch her. There was something mesmerizing in her jerking motions, in the muffled groans coming from inside the hood; it was hypnotic, like watching the flames in a fireplace. In fact, why shouldn't I have a fire for this? I got up and lit the simulated-wood fire, lowering the lights until the flames cast her bare, glistening skin in a flickering glow.

I was absolutely calm now and surprisingly happy with myself. Her muffled cries had become part of the room's ambiance, contrasting nicely with its soft leathers and dark wood. I had a vision of Jesse as a party decoration, naked, hooded, and hogtied on the table, writhing in the fire's glow as people stood around talking with their drinks in hand.

I got up and removed the hood; I wanted to see her eyes.

Without it and its built-in loop, though, I needed to tie a strap around her forehead to keep her head up, which I did. She tried to say something while this was going on, but the leather gag made her grunts incomprehensible. No matter, I could tell from the mix of pain and rage in her eyes that she wasn't happy.

In fact, it was even better for me that she was still acting like a wildcat. I wasn't totally sure that I could handle it if she were to become normal again, to plead with me. Reaching into the bag I found the piranhas and held them in front of her face. For a flickering second her rage was replaced by fear. Good, she was finally beginning to understand that she had gone too far with me. Pushing her back by the shoulders I grabbed each breast and slipped the piranhas on as far as they would go. A high-pitched groan came from her throat as they bit into her nipples. Then I slowly lowered her to the floor until her full weight was back on them. Now, every time she moved the piranhas pushed against the hardwood floor and took a new bite. She tried to arch her back higher to take the weight off, but it was impossible, and slowly she resigned herself to their gnawing pain.

I stared into her eyes. I could see that the pain in her nipples was gradually being overshadowed by that in her arched back and shoulders. I realized that each new pain had its own unique time and personality - more useful information.

I watched her suffer like this for almost five minutes. Gradually the rage in her eyes was replaced by an unmistakable plea for mercy; the same look she had given me in the airport lounge. I ignored her for another full minute. Finally I reached over and released the strap that held her in the hogtie, and her body un-flexed, prone and motionless on the floor. She groaned as her over-stressed muscles relaxed, and I removed her gag.

She lay exhausted on her front. Her wrists and crossed ankles were still bound and the piranhas were still clamped to her punished nipples. I examined her hands and feet carefully to be sure that there was no loss of circulation, and spoke to her in a voice devoid of all emotion.

'Are you ready to talk to me normally now?' I asked.

I'm not sure what I expected, but it wasn't the voice dripping with venom that snapped, 'No, Howard the Coward. I'll bet you enjoyed every minute of that.'

I was surprised and it showed in my face, and she took my surprise as a minor victory and smiled. But every victory has its price. Without hesitation I reinserted the gag and pulled her back into the arch for another five minutes, her suffering this second time even more excruciating.

When I released the gag she sobbed hysterically, unable to catch her breath. As before, her wrists and ankles were still tied and the piranhas were still in place. I wanted her to believe that I was ready to do it again. I watched her with mixed emotions - on one hand she deserved it, in spades; on the other, did anyone have the right to cause this much pain in another human being, for any reason? I didn't know the answer; all I knew was that I needed to come out of this contest a clear winner, for both our sakes.

When the crying subsided I said, 'I can keep this up all night, Jess, how about you?' There was real apprehension in her eyes now.

'Listen to me. I fully intend to emancipate you as soon as I can. But until that happens I need you to act like a human being. I can't have you making scenes, or threatening me, or stealing my keys, or pissing on my grandfather's rug. So it seems to me that the only way I can prevent those things is to temporarily exert my legal rights over you as your contract owner, and for you to act like the CELT that you are.'

I paused; there was no answer from her. I was frustrated. Did she really want me to do it again? Then I realized my mistake. CELTs speak only when invited, typically in response to a direct question.

'Do you agree to act like my contract-girl until I emancipate you?' I asked.

'Yes, Master,' she said respectfully. This time I didn't correct her. I really was her master, at least for a while. It would be better if we both remembered that.

Gently I removed the piranhas and untied her. Then I lowered her arms and retied them behind her back. I wanted to be sure she was herself. She didn't move or make a sound. After a while I helped her to her knees. Then I sat back down in my chair. She was naked with her hands tied, sitting back on her haunches in the firelight. She was incredibly beautiful. Slowly she raised her head and looked at me. Her mouth was partly open and I could see her tongue moving between her teeth. She was breathing heavily. Her pointed nipples looked amazing.

'You owe me a kiss, Howard,' she said softly.

It took me a moment to understand. Then I remembered her challenge at dinner to turn me into a sadist within an hour. Was that only an hour ago?

'Look, Jesse, we need to talk about...'

She interrupted me. 'No more talk, Howard. My kiss...'

I stood up and walked over to her. Then I reached under her arms and lifted her to her feet. We looked at each other and then kissed eagerly as I ran my hands over her naked, bound body.

At some point she dropped to her knees and started to nuzzle my crotch. I stepped out of my clothes. She moved to me on her knees and turned her head sideways, gently sucking my balls into her mouth. I could feel her teeth and mouth pressing softly as her throat made a low purring sound. I was instantly ready to come, but I held back determinedly, knowing this was not the right moment.

After a time she took my cock into her mouth. As I had imagined she was accomplished and used her lips and tongue to massage and stimulate me, and I pushed my cock deeply into her throat. It was necessary to pull back occasionally to give her time to breathe, but eventually we found the right rhythm and soon it seemed as natural as fucking her pussy.

At exactly the right moment her eyes lifted and I knew that, for the moment at least, she was subjugated. It was an incredible moment of insight. She was fulfilled, helpless, on her knees, sucking my cock. This was not a conscious or voluntary act; it was the result of fifty thousand years of human evolution.

I felt an incredible rush of strength and power and grabbed her hair in both hands as

I came in her mouth; every muscle in my body straining. She didn't choke or struggle to pull away. Just the opposite, her body began undulating as she hungrily swallowed every drop.

I kept her hands tied and carried her to her room, laying her gently on the bed. She wasn't asleep, but she wasn't fully conscious either. It was a kind of stupor, almost as if she were drugged. That night I kept her tied and fucked her, and then I freed her and went to my room.

The next morning I left early again, before she was awake. I left her all the cash I had in the house, about $1,500, and a very different kind of note.

Jesse,

I'm not sure exactly what happened last night, but it was incredibly wonderful. I would love to have you as my CELT, whatever the consequences. However, I also want you to stay of your own accord. Consequently, I reaffirm my promise to emancipate you with no financial penalty if you so choose.

We can talk about it when I get home.

The money enclosed is a gift for clothes and other essentials you may need.

Sincerely,

Howard Lowe

July 15, 2115

CHAPTER SIX

The library in my grandfather's house was large, about thirty feet long and twenty feet wide with a peaked ceiling. Crisscrossed beams ran the full length of the ceiling, creating voids which looked like the night sky when the lighting was right. A beautiful dark oak had been used to finish all surfaces and to trim the fireplace, which was made of rough-cut black granite. A large parlor and a dining room further isolated the library from the street. It was totally soundproofed, as my grandfather had intended.

Despite its size, the room was surprisingly cozy. This was achieved by creating three distinct zones. At one end there was an oversized cherry-wood desk; at the other was a long reading table made of the same light cherry. In the middle, in front of the fireplace, was the most unusual piece in the house - a huge coffee table made of the same rough-hewn black granite as the fireplace. The table's stone surface seemed to absorb light, creating an inky black hole in the floor. Its enormous weight was supported by a number of steel beams which rose up out of a concrete platform in the base.

I arrived home that evening with mixed emotions. What had been inconceivable twenty-four hours ago was now an undeniable truth - I was capable of sadism. And more importantly, as Jesse had predicted, I'd enjoyed it!

This had been on my mind all day. I knew now that her previous threats were hollow. It had just been another part of her game, one designed to feed on my insecurity. I was beginning to realize that Jesse was an expert at finding and pushing the right buttons.

She had, in fact, scripted the entire evening, including her punishment. It was amazing how easily I had been manipulated, and I was resolved that tonight would be different. I'd be a perfect gentleman and I'd force her to be a perfect lady, assuming, of course, she had decided to stay. I was sure we could work out a more normal relationship, something that made sense for both of us. I had even prepared a little speech of apology. I still didn't want people to know that I now owned a CELT, but I was no longer prepared to give her up just for that reason.

She was waiting for me in the library. After last night's pissing scene I was sure that nothing she could do would ever surprise me again. But I was wrong.

She was kneeling on the stone coffee table naked, except for a hood and a collar. The collar, which was tied to an overhead beam, kept her upper body ramrod straight. A wooden platform of some kind held her feet and legs motionless. The light-absorbing surface of the table made it appear that she was floating.

A mean-looking riding crop and two leather mittens lay neatly on the table beside her. Three complete dinner outfits had been arranged on the nearby easy chairs. The fourth chair, the one closest to her, was empty.

I was struck dumb and walked around the table in a trance. I sat down to think and, I admit, to study her amazing bondage.

The kneeler resting on the table was an antique made of light oak. Surprisingly it fitted quite well with the room's decor. She must have been out specifically to buy it. It was two inches thick, about three feet long and two feet wide. Her upturned feet lay absolutely flat about twelve inches apart inside two beautifully carved indentations. A second wooden block, with holes in the shape of a heel, held the back of her feet. This block was hinged to the base like a stock. I could see that the foot indentations in the surface were designed to hold her feet in place while the block was being closed; this would be important, I thought, if she was struggling. A thin leather strap completed the binding. It prevented the feet from moving laterally or curling up, but still allowed them to arch beautifully.

At the other end of the base was a thick leather kneeling pad. Straps buckled just behind the knees, forcing them deep into the leather and keeping them about twenty inches apart. It was clear that the purpose of spreading her knees was to expose the full length of her inner thighs and her cunt to the whip. I imagined that her terror was greatly increased by being so open and exposed.

This was a working bastinado - a torture device popular for centuries to exert control, especially over mistresses or sexually repressed young wives. After a night of unsatisfactory sex, for example, a gentleman would sometimes have his lady dress properly and then lock her in the bastinado. When he returned in the evening he would cane the soles of her feet to motivate better performance. During the day the bound victim could continue to supervise the affairs of the household, and even receive her consoling friends. If a harsh caning left her unable to walk that evening, all the better; her first place was in bed anyway.

Jesse also wore a black leather hood that hugged every curve of her beautiful face. It had two small holes for breathing through the nose, and a larger hole for her mouth. The black ball-gag from Max's bag was strapped deep inside her mouth, making her full lips appear even fuller.

Stretching her neck to its limit was a six inch leather collar. It had a cruel blunt point at the top which pushed against the underside of her jaw, forcing her head high and back. Six tiny buckles in the front were used to tighten the device, and there was a metal D-ring in the back that allowed the collar to be used as a general purpose attachment point.

The rope that hung from the ceiling beam was no ordinary clothesline. It was a black, non-stretch climber's rope. It had been tied to the collar's D-ring, run over the overhead beam, and then tied off to the D-ring with a non-slip climber's knot. It was obvious from her straight back that her upper body had been pulled taunt by the rope before it was tied off. Jesse obviously liked her bondage tight.

Her wrists were also secured to the collar with a double-sided snap hook. She must have done this by bending each arm back to the shoulder blade and then snapping the hook on to the collar's D-ring - an incredibly awkward and painful maneuver.

Clearly she'd put herself in this position, but what did it mean? Was this her way of communicating her decision to stay; to reaffirm her status as my CELT? I thought about this for several minutes. Maybe, but there was something else; she also wanted to test me, make sure that last night was no fluke. I was sure of it; she wanted to see how I would respond when there was no anger or emotion involved. I was instantly glad that my apology remained my secret; this girl had no time for weak men.

But how was I going to respond? Was I strong enough? What if I didn't measure up? What if I looked like a weakling? For a minute the insecurity and fear were overwhelming, then I felt another emotion, an even stronger one - anger. Who was she to be testing me!

I retrieved the mittens, stepped onto the table and moved behind her with my legs astride the bastinado. I closed her hands into fists and strapped on the leather mittens. I could feel her body trembling through her fingers. Did I have the strength to hurt her? My anger disappeared instantly and I felt my resolve eroding. She was incredibly beautiful; could I really whip her... in cold blood?

My hands were shaking as I moved to her front and tightened the six straps on her collar, forcing her head up even higher. This also made her back straighter, putting a little slack into the rope, which I retightened until it was like a guitar string.

Her body now formed a perfect 'L'. She could move her hips and flat belly a few inches in either direction, but that was it, otherwise it was as if she was set in concrete. She was also absolutely silent. I stepped down from the table and sat back in the chair. Cruelly I considered adding the piranhas. No, I thought, I didn't want her distracted. For the next half-hour or so I wanted her mind totally focused on the crop... and on me.

I picked up the clothes she had laid out and held each one up to her front. She bristled as the material brushed her bare skin. I selected a white silk shirt with a plunging neckline and a gray skirt. She had included some underwear which I set aside; tonight I wanted her naked beneath the clothes. For shoes I selected a pair of ultra-sexy ankle-strap heels.

Holding the shirt against her body I made tiny dots on her skin with a felt-tipped pen from my desk. I did the same with the skirt. These marked the areas covered by the clothes I'd selected. I'm sure she knew what was happening. It must feel strange, I thought, to know you were being prepared for pain.

Taking a deep breath I picked up the crop and made a few test swipes. I had never beaten a woman, but the crop felt natural in my hand as I moved into a comfortable whipping position.

I struck her ass. There was a satisfying 'thwack' and her body jerked, but she made no sound. I struck her a second time, harder, and then a third until I heard a muffled yelp. This was the right level of force, so I started again.

Each stroke produced a red mark which made an ideal guide as I moved down her thighs in neat rows. She was glistening with sweat when I'd finished. Then without hesitating I started on her inner thighs. This was serious pain and immediately her yelps and jerks changed into short screams and mini convulsions. I watched closely to gauge the force needed for maximum pain. After a while the swish of the crop, the satisfying *thwack*, her muffled screams and physical jerks all blended into a kind of savage rhythm.

When I finished her thighs I moved to the front and paused. She was moaning pitifully. I thought about removing her gag, but decided to wait.

I worked my way down her torso, taking care to avoid her breasts and cunt lips, and always staying within the tiny black dots. When I was finished I stood back and watched her again. Her body moved in a dance of intense pain, as if engulfed in flame.

I removed the gag and stood back. She immediately started panting heavily, too overwhelmed even to scream. I almost stopped the proceedings, but then I remembered she was testing me. What would she think if I ended her torment too early? So I stood back and viciously lashed her breasts, leaving her nipples to the end. Her head twisted violently and she wailed in agony with each new stroke. I heard her try to mutter 'please' a number of times, but she never quite got the word out. I replaced her gag, amazed at my growing callousness.

Then I whipped her cunt, and could see her mind shutting down, a self-defense response to the excruciating torment.

No, I wanted her to feel every stroke. I sat down and relaxed, giving her time to recover, and when she calmed a little I stood again and gave the sole of each foot five test strokes. The bastinado worked perfectly to hold her feet absolutely still. I knew somehow that this was the only pain that would now penetrate to her brain. There was no sound from her anymore and the only real movement was the tensing and un-tensing of her ass cheeks. I used this to gauge the pain and the timing of each stroke, knowing that she would only feel new strokes now when the pain subsided. As I waited I watched the mittens ripple as her fingers moved in an instinctive yet futile attempt to claw through the leather to release the snap hooks restraining her wrists.

I wanted her to still be able to walk, so I cropped her feet to that limit, which somehow I knew. Then I dropped my pants, stepped up on the table, and removed her gag. Without waiting I grabbed the back of her hooded head and fed my cock into her mouth, but her mind had shut down and there was almost no response.

Leaning over her head slightly I began to savagely crop her ass and thighs again. This new cropping on top of the old shocked her out of her stupor. Almost immediately she understood the relationship between her new pain and the cock in her mouth, and started to frantically suck me off. This was the desperate act of a creature in pain, with none of the artful finesse of the evening before, but it did the job equally well and unfortunately I ejaculated all too soon.

Feeling a little short-changed I adjusted my pants and returned to the chair. The girl was covered with livid welts that must have burned like the fires of hell. Curious, I watched her toned and tensed muscles twitching for many quiet, almost peaceful, minutes. Then I stood again and ran my hands over her hot and sweating body. At first she pulled away, afraid, but gradually she began to respond, pushing herself against my moving fingers. Incredibly, I got the message that she wanted to be fucked again.

But I had other plans for the evening, so carefully I released her from all the bondage and laid her down on the black table next to the bastinado. After a few minutes' rest she began to stir, and I spoke for the first time.

'Take this outfit, Jesse,' I indicated the one I'd selected, 'and go shower. We're going out to dinner. You have one hour to recover yourself and get ready. If you're not back here by then we'll repeat the cropping.' I knew this was the appropriate tone. I waited, and slowly, gingerly, she raised herself, swung her legs off the table and sat on its edge, and winced as she carefully placed her feet on the floor.

'Go and get ready,' I told her.

She tried to get to her feet, but they were too tender. She tried again and again, but was unable to put any weight on them. My natural instinct was to move to her aid, but I fought to remain aloof, watching. Finally she clamped the clothes and shoes between her neat white teeth and slowly left the room on her hands and knees with feline grace, despite her distress.

Once she was gone a wave of shame washed over me. What had I done? She had wanted it, but did that make it right? Did anything give me the right to treat her that way?

Oh, fuck it. This was no time for moral confusion, for weakness. I was convinced she was testing my mettle, and there was no way I was going to come up short again.

CHAPTER SEVEN

Jesse returned to the library with five minutes to spare, walking uncomfortably but steadily to the door in her high heels. Perfect, I thought; just enough pain to remind her that I could be harsh as well as kind.

She looked stunning, with an amazing glow I'd never before seen in a woman. Was it the whipping?

Her hair was tied in a single long braid, exposing the graceful sweep of her neck, and the chosen clothes molded to her shapely contours perfectly.

I took her arm and led her to the front door, where I helped with her coat. Then I held out my arm and she took it without hesitation.

'Outside this door, you will speak and act like my girlfriend. Inside you will do nothing without my permission. Is that clear?' She smiled contentedly and nodded her head in understanding. I waited for the proper response, suspecting she was still testing me.

'Yes, Master, I understand,' she replied politely, after a few seconds. I nodded and carefully walked us outside to the waiting cab.

After giving instructions to the driver I turned to her and asked, 'Where did you get the clothes?'

'Two different shops on Fifth, Mas...' she stopped and looked at me with a mischievous smile, '...Howard.' I smiled in return, amazed at her recuperative ability; an hour ago she was incoherent with pain.

'And the bastinado?' I whispered.

'From a dealer I know in the village,' she replied, seemingly surprised that I knew its name.

'It's an excellent piece,' I said. 'You'll have to give me his name and address. I may want to buy more pieces from him.'

'I will,' she said. 'I'm happy you're pleased. It's actually somewhat rare. Eighteenth century, he told me.'

'U-huh,' I mused. 'The bastinado was popular at that time in Eastern Europe and the Middle East. Did you know it was primarily used in the home to train sexually repressed young girls?' I was speaking too softly for the driver to hear. She shook her head and looked at me directly for the first time.

'Sometimes men wanted more from their women. Girls in those days were often too shy to even raise their nightgowns,' I explained. 'Proper young ladies of the day, even mistresses, were programmed to resist for as long as they could. They were actually a lot more comfortable with being forced to submit, especially for "despicable acts". You could say that the bastinado was making things easier for everyone. Judging from its condition I'd say the one you bought has been in steady use since it was made.'

'Its condition?' She was openly curious, and intrigued by what I was able to tell her.

'Yes, the dark marks where the feet are tied; I'm sure they're blood mixed with sweat. In the old days they used a cane and they weren't too worried about drawing a little blood. Probably hundreds of girls have bled on that wood.' I could see she was listening intently.

'It took a long time for women to get some rights,' she said pensively.

'Yes it did,' I concurred, 'then as soon as the CELT laws came into effect thousands of them sold those rights off to the highest bidder.' I could see that she wanted to respond, but held back. I stayed quiet as well. The last thing we needed tonight was a political debate.

'Did you spend all the money?' I asked casually.

She looked at me, and I could see she was trying to think of a right answer, and then eventually she just said, 'Yes,' and looked down guiltily, adding, '...and a little more. The owner of the shop said I could pay him the rest later.'

I looked at her and nodded. 'I'll send him a check for what we owe, but please don't spend my money again without asking.' She looked relieved by my response.

In truth this was not acceptable behavior for a CELT. Most owners would have severely punished such irresponsible buying behavior, but I let it drop. There were things I needed to learn before exerting real authority, and there was also a more serious issue in her hesitation to respond to my question.

I looked at her with a hard expression. 'Don't ever think about hiding something like that from me again, okay?'

She nodded again, and smiled. Then impulsively she grabbed my hand and held it against her silk-clad breast. I could feel her hard nipple against the back of my hand. Clearly I had passed another test. We didn't speak for the rest of the short ride.

I had selected a quiet Italian restaurant on the lower east side. I knew they had great food and secluded corner booths, one of which I asked for.

Once seated I took her through the menu in detail, explaining the special way in which many of the dishes were prepared. I had been there many times, mostly with friends and business colleagues.

'I'm not that hungry, Howard,' she said. 'In fact, I'm pretty full.' She looked at me playfully and grinned, licking her lips. I chuckled, knowing exactly what she meant. That broke the ice, and we started talking again like friends. It was a repeat of the previous evening, and I marveled again at how quickly she had recovered from the earlier beating.

She steered most of our conversation back to life in the eighteenth century, specifically how men treated their women. I'm no expert, but I like to read history books and I know a fair bit about it, and she seemed happy to listen to me. And I was also happy that she was intellectually curious. That was important to me. I wanted to be with someone smart because dumb girls, even if they are gorgeous, turn me off.

But once the meal was served I broached the delicate subject of our relationship. 'What was that all about tonight, Jess?' I asked.

She didn't try to deflect the question, but her smile faded and she stared at her plate for a while. 'You told me to act like a CELT, Howard. That's what I was doing.' The open friendliness was gone; she was back in role. I had a flashback to the way she had spoken about Max, and it was the same tone as then.

'That's not good enough, Jess,' I replied. 'I'm not interested in having a CELT whore or a B&D fetishist on my hands; I want us to have a relationship, at least until we get you emancipated, if that's what you want.' She looked at me with a strange expression and nodded mechanically, but didn't say anything.

I have to admit that I was hurt by her silence. 'Let me ask you a question,' I went on. 'Do you feel anything for me?'

'Look, Howard,' she said, more warmly, 'why can't we just let it rest. I'm here as your CELT. I'm not a whore; I'm only here with one man. And I'm not sure about emancipation, but until we work that out I'll abide by the terms of my contract. There's no rush, is there? I love the time we've spent together... on both sides of your front door. And no, I'm not a B&D fetishist; I hate pain just like most people do. In fact I'm terrified of what is in store for me with you, but I'm a CELT and I've agreed to this... this arrangement. Can't we just let things stay as they are for a while?' She reached out across the table for my hand and squeezed it.

But her touch seemed mechanical, as if it was the right thing for an escort to do at that moment, and for some reason that enraged me. 'No,' I hissed, 'I don't accept your explanation or this situation.' She continued to hold my gaze, but withdrew her hand. 'I know part of this has been a game. I know you're not the kind of person who picks an argument with a waiter and then attacks him with a blueberry pie.' She lowered her eyes and blushed. 'You're also not the kind of person who pisses on a rug when you're angry.' Her blush got even deeper.

We were both quiet for a minute, and then she leaned back and started talking in a totally different manner. 'Okay, Howard, you want the truth so badly, here it is. Yes, I did manipulate things. That's what powerless CELTs do - we manipulate things. You helped me with Max and I wanted to repay the favor. I knew you were too nice a guy to do it on your own so I helped you out a bit to get us started. We both know you did great. But the hard truth is that it was just part of the game. How could it be anything more? We've only known each other a few days.'

She stopped for a minute, leaned back in and again took my hand in hers. 'I like you, Howard... a lot, but we're not in love,' she continued. 'Good men like you fall in love with their CELTs all the time.' Her voice dropped to a whisper. 'It's fairly understandable, after all, we've already been extremely intimate with each other, in many ways. But in truth it's all just part of our game, and frankly part of our business relationship. We can both get badly hurt by thinking it's something more.' She paused and looked around to be sure she was not being overheard.

'This is what most CELT arrangements are like. They are not about real love or subjugation or dominance. They are fantasies. A power relationship, a real one, is dangerous. There are so many emotions and feelings involved - pain, fear, love, hate, sex, desire, jealousy - that it takes someone with real experience to pull it off, someone with a stone heart.'

Then mercilessly she delivered the coup de grâce. 'You still want to emancipate me, dear Howard... how hard is your heart?'

I was devastated. Despite the craziness of the last few days I thought we actually had developed some kind of closeness for each other. I knew it wasn't love, but maybe it was... well, I don't know what it was. I only knew that I felt something and I didn't want it to end. I also didn't want us to mutate into a man and his beautiful CELT whore.

But what she said about the reality of our situation had the ring of truth, and that hurt. 'I need to think about this, Jess,' I said honestly. 'Let's go home.'

We rode home in silence, then I walked her to her bedroom.

'Maybe we could sleep together tonight, Howard?' she asked meekly, obviously upset over the night's turn of events. 'That was nice last night, and I really don't want to be alone now.'

'I don't think so, Jesse,' I answered. Then I kissed her gently on the cheek and walked along the landing to my own room, feeling horribly empty. I was aware that she stood in the open doorway of her room until my door closed, and then I heard hers quietly shut too. It all seemed very sad.

I didn't sleep much that night, or the next four. Each morning I left early and returned very late, working hard to avoid any real contact with her. A number of times she tried to initiate conversation, but it was obvious I was sulking, and after a while she just stayed out of my way.

The sixth night I made preparations, and the next day I called the bank to say I was sick with the flu.

CHAPTER EIGHT

I was waiting for her when she opened her bedroom door. She was barefoot, dressed in jeans and a sweatshirt. Her hair was wet and she had a wonderful, just-showered smell.

'Howard, I...' she started when she saw me waiting.

'Strip,' I said.

'Howard, I think...' she tried again.

'Strip!' I barked, in a voice that would have made a marine drill instructor proud.

She stared at me for a few seconds, and then she obediently peeled off her sweater and stepped out of her jeans. She was wearing the black thong she had worn in the airport. 'Leave that,' I said as she started to remove it. 'Turn around and put your hands behind your back.' I was surprised at how steady my voice was.

She turned around and obeyed. I quickly cuffed her wrists with leather shackles and pulled the leather hood over her head. I buckled it behind her neck, and she stood there almost naked and tall, an obedient CELT; no sound, no movement, no false modesty. I took her arm and led her past the library, and down steps to the cellar. There was a faint hesitation in her body when we started down the cold, stone cellar steps, but no resistance.

In front of us was the house's safe room - a concrete chamber about twelve feet square. It had been used during the food riots of the 2080s, and apart from the visit I'd made to it that morning to make the necessary modifications, no one had been in it for some time.

I led her through the doorway and stood her in the room's center. There was total and absolute silence. It was a tomb, and the outside sounds of everyday life couldn't penetrate the walls.

Leaving her hood in place I moved her wrists to her front and tied them to the rope hanging from the ceiling. It ran through the eye hook I'd installed for this purpose, and I pulled her arms up until her hands were just above her head. Then I attached leather ankle cuffs to her feet and snapped them on to a short chain I had bolted to the floor.

I removed her hood and moved back into the shadows. She looked around the room, giving her eyes time to adjust to the light. The track-mounted spotlights in the ceiling were all centered on her naked form.

'It's called a safe room,' I said from the dark corner. 'It has one foot of reinforced concrete all around with a four inch steel-core door. There's a small bathroom in the back. It was built during the food riots for protection against home invasion. In case you're interested, these walls also support the fireplace and the stone table you like in the library.'

She looked around the empty concrete room, but didn't say anything. 'It's completely soundproof, of course,' I continued, 'like the library. I guess my grandfather really liked his privacy.'

She remained silent, waiting.

'I decided that you were right last night, Jess. Everything that's happened in the last few days has been basically a game. You played a little; I played a little; we had some fun, but it's certainly not the basis of a relationship... of any kind.' She was looking in the direction of my voice now, shifting her weight from one foot to another, apparently unconcerned. 'It did however give me a taste for the power you mentioned, so I've decided to explore that a little.'

'Howard, can I say something?' It was the tone of a wise friend about to give advice, and it was rather annoying.

'No. You can't speak right now, Jess, but I'll give you some time in a few minutes.' I was trying to sound equally reasonable and mature. 'In fact, let's start with the rules for this room. You may not speak in here except in response to a direct question. That applies to the rest of the house as well, but every word you say in this room will cost you one stroke of the whip. Please don't test me on this; I'd hate to lose a day of my program whipping you for a speaking violation. Second, in this room you may not ask for permission to speak. You will be permitted to do that respectfully in the rest of the house, but not here. Third, just for your information, this room is only for discipline, we will never have sex in here.'

She was looking a little bored, but I suspected this was more CELT psycho-manipulation. I waited a few minutes before continuing. I needed to learn her tricks if I was to really master her.

'I've also decided that you were right about my lack of resolve. I knew exactly what I wanted from the moment I laid eyes on you; I just couldn't admit it even to myself.' She looked even more bored, and now I was sure it was manipulation. And it was rather good, designed to evoke anger and poor judgment.

I ignored the subtle provocation and continued. 'I want you, Jess. I'm not totally sure what that means right now, but I know that I don't want to free you. I never really wanted to do that, I just thought it was the right thing, something I was expected to do. I also have no intention of selling you... your contract, that is, and I certainly have no intention of allowing you to run my life.'

I stopped and waited. 'But this conversation is for later; right now all you need to know is that I am exercising my legal right under our contract to use corporal punishment to correct your behavior - behavior I consider unacceptable. As per the contract and the laws governing CELT arrangements, there will be no lasting affects, physical or mental, from this discipline. I've written this down and mailed it to my lawyer along with a copy of our contract. You have the right to notify your lawyer independently if you want.

'Do you understand this right?' I asked. She looked amused and nodded. 'Do you want to call your lawyer?' She shook her head. Despite my new understanding that this was all part of her act, I was getting annoyed with the smartass smirk on her face.

This legal formula was just a formality, but it was necessary before any serious long term disciplinary action could take place. My lawyer would send a notice to hers, or at least the lawyer identified in her contract, who was supposed to file a watch-notice with the police. It was intended to prevent abuse, but it was never enforced. It just made me feel a little better to be complying with the law.

'Do you want to say anything for the record before we start?' I asked.

'Howard, our contract doesn't require me to fuck you and it certainly does not require me to love you, yet we both know that's what you want.'

But she was wrong. Our previous discussion had shown me that love was much too ambiguous. Right now all I wanted was respect.

But all I said was, 'Should I write that down?' She shook her head, still wearing that maddeningly condescending smile. I was now convinced that she was putting on an act. In fact, it occurred to me that her attitude was getting tougher as she became more uneasy, and I almost lost my nerve with that realization.

Instead I tried to explain. 'Despite my recent ineptitude, Jess, most of what I did was driven by an honest desire to show you kindness, even friendship. You basically dismissed that as weakness and manipulated me into becoming your partner in a sex and bondage game. I admit that I was a willing participant, but I deserved more; I deserved some genuine emotion from you.'

35

Her smirk disappeared. 'And since you place so little value on what I did, I've decided to carry out the punishment Max had set for you, which I'm sure you remember.'

Her eyes widened and for a second I could see that I was right - she was terrified, but disciplined enough to remain silent. I remembered her words from the other night, 'powerless CELTs manipulate things.'

'You may speak now if you want to,' I said.

'It won't work, Howard,' she said calmly. The mask was back; she was desperately hiding her fear. 'You don't have it in you, and when you discover the truth of that you're going to be scarred for life.' She was using her most convincing and persuasive tone.

'You call it a game,' she said, 'but it felt good to me and I know it felt good to you. Let's just start with that. I don't care about being emancipated. I never wanted anything from you that I didn't deserve. I still don't. Take me upstairs, whip me then fuck my brains out. I know you like it that way; it's your right. A lot of things can happen in a year.' She stopped; there were no tears in her eyes and no fear in her face, but in the harsh light I could see her breathing hard.

I moved and stood in front of her naked body. 'You're wrong, Jess,' I replied gently. 'A whore is just a whore, no matter how beautiful or smart. Believe me, I know a lot of them. Most of my friends are married to whores. You're better than that. I know it and I'm going to prove it.'

She looked at me with pity.

'Anything else?' I asked, and defiantly she shook her head. I knew she wanted to beg me not to hurt her, but was too proud. I admired that. I walked over to the rope and lifted her arms until she was on her toes. Then I stood in front of her again, eye to eye.

'I feel sorry for you, Howard,' she said, still hiding her fear. I recognized the sincerity in her comment and wondered again if I could actually pull this off.

'That's five extra strokes,' I replied, and she just looked at me. I stepped back into the shadows.

Max's electric whip was a single-tail horror with copper wire woven through the braid. That morning I whipped her for half an hour with the setting on #1, the lowest. It was as if she were being shocked with a cattle prod and touched with a red-hot iron at the same time.

She screamed and thrashed wildly after each stroke, but I was patient, waiting until she was fully recovered and calm before delivering the next. Near the end she was fading in and out of consciousness, so to be sure she felt the last few strokes I wet her down and brushed her skin with the whip. The shock of it revived her enough to allow me to finish.

When it was over I lowered her arms about a foot and gave her some water through a straw.

I waited ten minutes for her to rest, then I collared her and attached a four foot chain, which I locked at her feet. The chain forced her to bend at the knee with her arms extended overhead. The only way to give her straining leg muscles some relief was to either bend at the waist, which caused a terrible back pain, or to hang by her wrists.

I wanted her to spend the day shifting from one agony to another. I also wanted to strengthen her muscles, especially in her legs; she would need them later.

Without a word I turned off all the lights but one, and left, locking the door behind me.

That evening I returned. She was crying softly from the pain of her bondage. From the door peephole I knew that her back and legs had given out two hours earlier and she'd been hanging by her arms since then, pushing up periodically with her trembling legs to ease the discomfort.

She looked at me and started to sob in relief; all she could think about now was the pain. I was her salvation. I unhooked the chain from her neck collar and watched as she tried to stand straight. She didn't have enough strength left in her legs. After a minute I lowered her to the floor and fed her water, a baloney sandwich, and two protein bars.

She ate slowly, mechanically, then I locked her wrists behind her back and hooked her collar to the short chain in the floor. Her face was lying in the wet spot where she had peed during the day. I closed the lights and left.

The next morning I returned, increased the whip's setting to #2 and whipped her for another half-hour. Afterwards I shortened the neck chain by one link and put her back in position. I knew her tolerances would increase and I wanted to be sure that each day's pain was just about the same.

This went on for five days. I don't know if Max would have whipped her for seven, and I didn't really care. I was now in charge and I had decided that she'd had enough.

As far as Jesse was concerned it didn't matter either. Her life was now defined by a morning whipping, a day of excruciating pain, and a long uncomfortable sleep in the tomb-like darkness. Already she didn't know if this had gone on for five days or fifty.

I moved her to the soft bed upstairs where she slept for thirty-six hours. When she eventually woke I shackled her hands and gave her a bath, then I fed her a hot meal and put her back to bed. She was as weak as a kitten and never looked at me directly, or said a word. She slept for another twenty-four hours and I repeated the bath and meal routine. Again she was silent throughout.

If nothing else, I now had her attention.

CHAPTER NINE

I was waiting the next morning when she opened her bedroom door, just as I had been a week before. Again she was barefoot, dressed in jeans and a sweatshirt, with wet hair. She stopped when she saw me waiting. She still looked weak, but surprisingly healthy.

'How are you feeling?' I asked.

'Fine, Master,' she answered, head bowed as I looked her over. My arms were crossed and I was leaning against the landing balustrade.

'Strip,' I again said quietly, and this time she immediately removed her clothes, leaving the thong in place without being told to. I was amazed at her instantaneous, unquestioning response. Obviously there was fear involved - she didn't want to go back to the safe room - but there was something more, much more. She had obeyed me without thinking... instinctively, and I was beginning to understand what she meant by a power relationship.

I circled her, reaching out to feel the toned muscles in her arms and thighs. I was especially impressed with her flat stomach and abs, which showed just a faint hint of the hardness underneath. I had the distinct impression of velvet-covered metal, yet nothing was bulging.

Her torments had been designed to harden existing muscle rather than build ugly bulk. Silently I congratulated myself. I didn't think it was possible, but she looked even better than before, even more desirable. I could feel myself getting hard.

'Dress,' I ordered, and immediately she put her clothes back on. 'You look even more beautiful than I've seen you look before,' I said, and saw a faint smile lighten her face. I returned to leaning against the balustrade with my arms crossed, while she stood straight, with her head bowed meekly and her hands at her sides.

'I'm going away on a business trip for a few days,' I said in a conversational tone. 'I'll be back late on Friday. I've left you some money on my desk. There's plenty of food in the kitchen.'

I waited a few moments and then continued. 'You can come and go as you like until I get back. You're free to use anything in the house, including the computer, just don't touch anything in my desk.'

She remained silent. 'On Saturday morning we'll be driving upstate. I've arranged for you to get some specialized training. You'll be gone for two weeks. Do you understand?'

She raised her head and looked at me curiously, but just responded with a quiet, 'Yes, Master.'

I guess I had hoped for a change in attitude, but sadly I realized that was asking too much. She could not act respectfully and with familiarity at the same time. Being a real master was going to be lonely.

'I made you some coffee downstairs,' I said. Then I turned and went back to my room and finished packing.

When I went downstairs she was waiting for me by the front door, naked except for the thong, and kneeling with her head down. She looked incredible, and it took all the willpower I had not to fuck her right there on the floor. Instead I stepped around her kneeling body to get my jacket.

'May I speak, Master?' she asked. This was the first time she had asked to speak since the basement.

'Yes,' I replied.

Then she looked up at me and said simply, 'Please fuck me before you go.' It was genuine sexual hunger, but there was something more. Behind the sex was a barely hidden plea to give her back some of the control she had lost, to help restore some of her pride.

After a week of manhandling her naked body there was nothing I wanted more than to fuck her, but I knew that giving in now would be a step back. I was resolved to stick to the plan, which meant no sex for a while.

'No, not yet,' I said in a matter-of-fact way. Then, without looking at her, I added, 'Please be ready to leave at ten on Saturday morning.' Then I left.

CHAPTER TEN

On Saturday morning the drive upstate took three hours, plus an hour for lunch at a little restaurant just off the Taconic Parkway. I had given her permission to speak freely and we talked - nothing important or intimate, but it was a start.

She asked me again how I knew so much about the bastinado, clearly fascinated with the subject. I told her that I had studied a lot of history, both in school and since.

'Who were the cruelest people?' she asked innocently, obviously enjoying her meal.

'The Romans,' I answered without hesitation. 'They institutionalized cruelty. Before them it was all about people - good people and bad. After them it became a government thing. It wasn't personal anymore and people absolved themselves of responsibility.

'You've heard of Spartacus and the slave revolt?' I asked. She nodded, but her eyes urged me to continue. The Romans crucified six thousand slaves and no one batted an eyelash. Do you know how much organization it took to get six thousand strong men nailed to a cross one at a time? Imagine waiting for your turn. Imagine thinking about the horribly painful death that was coming.

'I know how they felt,' she said, half-joking. I looked at her sharply; I didn't want her punishments to be taken lightly.

'We can do that again when we get home.' I said seriously. There was real alarm in her eyes. 'Do you want that?' I asked.

'No, Master,' she replied, cowed. I hated to bring that tone to our civilized lunch, but I knew that she needed to respect the pain I gave her, not diminish it once it was over.

'The Romans were particularly cruel to their slaves, especially the girls,' I continued, and she looked at me with interest, still wary about saying the wrong thing. 'The most beautiful became a secondary form of money and were traded all the time. It actually resulted in better treatment as marking a female slave reduced her value. They still practiced corporal punishment, but carefully, always looking for new ways to discipline the slave without damaging her. It became a hobby for some.'

She looked at me pensively, and then screwed up her courage and spoke. 'It sounds very much like a CELT contract. Men trade the girls and try to find inventive ways to keep them in line without any visible damage.' She was staring at me directly. There was no disrespect, but she stood her ground and once again I admired her courage.

I was also glad to see that she had not lost her spirit, but I just looked at her evenly and said, 'There's one important difference Jess - a CELT's bondage is consensual.'

'Yes, you're right,' she agreed. 'Consensual.' Then she stood up and walked out to the car. I paid the bill and followed.

CHAPTER ELEVEN

The sign read *Bitter Wells Horse Farm*. It was remote, at least twenty miles off the main road. This was horse country and I was sure that by now Jesse had guessed the nature of her training. She didn't say anything, just continued to stare out the window.

What could she say?

We drove up the farm road until we came to a collection of buildings, including a well-kept barn. A small group of men were gathered around something, but I couldn't see what it was. One of them broke away and walked over to the car.

'Mr Lowe?' the man asked in a friendly way. I nodded and we shook hands. 'Jack Warden,' he said. 'Welcome to Bitter Wells. I got your check and the paperwork last week. We're all set for you.' He didn't acknowledge Jess directly, who had gotten out of the car and walked around it to join us.

'Is this the girl?' he asked me, nodding indifferently in her direction.

'Yes,' I said.

'Do you want to turn her over now?' he asked, and again I answered my confirmation.

'Okay, well you just need to give her the order and we'll get started.'

So I turned to Jesse and said, 'I want you to obey this man and his associates.'

Then immediately he stepped to her, turned her around, and cuffed her wrists behind her back. Without a single wasted motion he pulled a bridle from his belt and fit it over her head, pushing a hard rubber bit between her teeth. Quickly he tightened one bridle strap behind her neck, another under her chin, and a third at the side of her head, and then he clipped two short reins to the metal ring on one side of her mouth bit. Two leather flaps near her eyes prevented any side vision.

Jesse stood motionless as the bridle was strapped on, staring at me. I stared back, betraying nothing of what I was feeling inside. In truth I was terrified of leaving her, and I knew that she was afraid as well. She had never been to a horse farm; I could see it in the way she responded clumsily to Jack's manhandling.

Then he unbuttoned the front of her shirt and pulled it down to her waist. 'We'll get her stripped down and prepared later,' he said. 'Right now I need to attend to one of our ponies. Want to watch?' I nodded, not really understanding what he meant by 'attend to.' He led Jesse away by the reins, and suddenly feeling uncomfortably out of my depth, I followed.

When we got closer I could see that the crowd was gathered around a horizontal wooden rail, maybe eight feet long, set on two thick posts. A tall Asian girl, completely naked and absolutely gorgeous, had been stretched over the rail on her stomach and her wrists and ankles pulled wide and secured by thick leather straps to the posts. Her head was pulled back by the hair with a rawhide cord that was tied to a silver hook, which had been plugged into her ass and held there by a narrow belt buckled tightly around her hips.

The leather straps secured to the posts pulled her lithe, sweating body taut and held it motionless. She strained to glance over at me, the new arrival in the circle, her eyes blazing with fury.

Jack continued walking to another hitching rail and pushed Jesse to her knees, tying her reins around the rail so that she was forced to look at the Asian girl. Five other girls were tied to the same rail in a similar fashion, all of them naked. A second rail nearby held another six 'ponies', all tied in the same kneeling position.

Jack addressed the small group of men. 'Thank you all for stopping by. Let me introduce Mr Lowe, here,' he gestured towards me with his open hand, and I nodded uncomfortably, '...our newest member.' Several of the men nodded and mumbled a gruff welcome.

Then Jack walked over to the punishment rail and rested his hand on the Asian girl's bare ass. 'This here's Ming,' he said, as he unhooked a mean looking rawhide whip from his belt and shook it to allow the lashes to untangle.

'Yesterday she pushed one of our stable boys. We don't tolerate behavior like that around here, so her subsequent punishment is to be whipped for ten minutes.' The girl remained resolutely silent and still, reminding me of Jesse in an obstinate mood.

He turned his address to the two hitching rails. 'I want all you other ponies to watch this and remember it well.'

He stepped slightly to the rear quarter of the bound girl and exercised the whip. For some reason she strained to look at me again, genuine trepidation in her eyes. Jack started slowly, moving the whip from one ass cheek to the other, each rawhide lash leaving a small red line on her smooth skin. After a few more strokes he shifted his attention to her legs, skillfully flicking the tips of the lash into the tender insides of her thighs. He concentrated on one leg, and then the other. The girl screamed and jerked with each accurate stroke, hopelessly trying to free herself from the rail. I glanced at my watch... only one minute had passed.

At the two minute mark her ass and back were bright, welted red and she was hysterical with the pain. She pleaded for him to stop, and surprisingly he did.

'I'll give her some time to calm down a little,' he told us onlookers. 'The break won't affect her allocated whipping time though; around here, ten minutes means ten minutes.'

The girl's body was shaking violently and tears were flowing down her flushed face in steady, meandering streams. I could see her hands desperately opening and closing and her bare feet arching as she tried to shake off the pain. Her face grimaced in agony as the punishment resumed and another blow landed, and I realized, surprised, shocked and somewhat ashamedly, that I was rock hard. I imagined she was suffering for me, and I found that secret fantasy incredibly exciting.

The exhausted girl was moaning and writhing again within a few strokes. I could tell that he was adjusting the force of the whipping so that she was in a fairly constant and intense pain, but not in danger of passing out. Strangely her protests seemed almost natural out here in the open air, with the rugged countryside and mountains as the backdrop. All the men were looking on with intense interest, eyes keen and lips being subconsciously licked. Obviously this was nothing new, but no less enjoyable for that.

I looked at the pony-girls strapped to the hitching rails. Some had their eyes closed, but some were watching intently and breathing heavily, and I realized that they were as turned on as the rest of us by the show - Jesse most of all.

By the end of her ten minutes poor Ming was barely conscious. Jack re-coiled his whip and reattached it to his belt. He turned to the gathered men. 'Thank you all for coming. It's good for the girls to see the membership working together. We'll release her in a few hours,' he said, nodding at Ming. 'I like them to think about what they've done while the hook is still plugged inside their ass and their backside is still raw and burning.'

The men started drifting away, and I took a final look at Ming. She was in a painful stupor, almost a drugged state, but her muscles were contracting as she squeezed the wooden rail with her legs. Was she having a surreptitious orgasm?

Jack came over and started walking me back to my car. 'We'll see you in two weeks,

41

Mr Lowe,' he said amiably, as though nothing had just occurred at all. 'And don't worry in the meantime; I'll take good care of your girl.'

I glanced over at Jesse, the wounded look in her eyes following me all the way down the path.

The next two weeks were the longest of my life. I realized two things: first, that I wanted Jesse more than anything I had ever wanted before; and second, just how dangerous it was to feel that way. It was a classic case of obsession, but fortunately I was smart enough to recognize the symptoms. And what was even more fortunate was that she was a hundred and fifty miles away.

The drive back to Bitter Wells was filled with anxiety and uncertainty. How had she responded to the training? The farm was all about humility; could Jesse learn humility... really learn it in her heart? I didn't know if she could, but what I did know was that the next few days would define our year together - if we had a year together.

After registering at the farm's guest quarters I wandered over to the clubhouse. Jack was seated at the bar drinking a cup of coffee.

'Hi, how are you, Mr Lowe?' he asked cheerfully, getting up to shake hands, signally me to sit on the stool next to his. 'Good trip?'

'Fine, thanks,' I said. 'How's my CELT?' I wanted to get down to business straight away.

'A little anxious to get back to your filly, huh?' he laughed. 'Don't blame you none, that's one incredibly beautiful girl you got there. And she's strong, too. I wouldn't have believed it, but underneath that beautiful skin she's got some hard-assed guts. You better watch yourself around her, especially now that we've been running her for a couple of weeks.'

I smiled and nodded. Actually I was jogging a lot farther than usual and playing tennis every day now, so I wasn't worried about being able to handle her.

'We did have some trouble with her at first, because she's got a kind of an independent streak. Most of the time we encourage that because spirited ponies are much better runners, but she just wouldn't obey. I had to put her on the rail a couple of times.' I frowned. 'Don't worry, I didn't make any marks,' he added quickly. 'She settled down a little after that, but I really couldn't tell if she was just going along to avoid the pain.' He took a few sips from his cup. 'You want some coffee... breakfast? I indicated no to both.

'Once we paired her up, though,' he continued, 'she calmed right down.' I could see that he enjoyed giving me a detailed report. 'Around here, when one member of a pair acts up they both get whipped. We tie them to the rail, one on top of the other and face-to-face. I guess she didn't like seeing her partner suffering for her bad behavior.

'They run pretty well together now. Thanks for your check, by the way. Your account's all paid up... until Tuesday.' He stopped and finished his coffee before continuing. 'Want to take her out for a run? Ever handled a team before?'

'I'd love to take her out,' I answered, 'and no, I've never done this before.'

'No problem, it's easy,' he replied. 'Today you can use the starter rig and just stick to the beginner's path. Your team can move along pretty well, but they're gentle for the most part. Give us another three weeks with your girl and we'll turn her into a fast quarter-miler.' I just smiled and shook my head. 'I don't blame you,' he said, 'but maybe you'll change your mind after you see her sprint tomorrow. There's money up here in girl racing, but I understand - she's a real beauty. First things first, let's just get you started for now.'

He led me outside and we walked to the stable.

Inside half a dozen girls were lined up, facing one wall. They were all bridled and chained to the wall by their mouth bits. Each had their hair in a ponytail, and their wrists were also shackled, pulled up hard behind their backs and tied tightly with rawhide, secured over the opposite shoulder to some point at their front that I couldn't see. A butt-plug had been inserted into each gorgeous ass and secured with a crotch strap. Horsehair, or what looked like horsehair, hung down from between their taut buttocks. They all wore strange, hoof-like shoes strapped to their feet.

Jesse was the third to the right. Standing next to her was the Asian girl who had been whipped the day I dropped Jesse off. Both of them were magnificent, standing tall and straight and proud.

Jack saw me staring at the shoes. 'They're called pony shoes,' he said, noting my interest. 'They arch the foot and transfer most of the ground shock to the leg just like a real horse. We also like them because they stretch their legs and raise their asses. What do you think?' He was right of course; they all looked incredibly beautiful, a little like Las Vegas showgirls. I nodded and smiled.

'You've met Ming before,' Jack said with a wry grin, running his hand down her back and flank as he talked. 'And you recognize this beauty, of course,' he said, as he gave Jess a playful spank on her toned ass. Jesse merely continued to stare at the wall.

'Well, I got to say she don't look all that happy to see you, Mr Lowe,' Jack observed. 'That's good, actually; she's high-strung and naturally miffed that you left her behind. Let's let her pout for a while.' I nodded. He had spoken in front of her as if she couldn't understand the meaning of his words, and I realized that this was part of the program - to dehumanize the girls.

'Let me show you how to hook them up,' he said, walking over to the opposite wall. 'This here's a body harness.' He lifted two leather harnesses off their hooks. They were made like the bridle, but much larger.

He moved back to Jesse and Ming, unhooked the bit chains that held both girls against the wall, and turned them around. I looked into Jesse's eyes, but she refused to meet my gaze. Then I looked down at their breasts. The wrist shackles were attached to their nipples, which had been pierced vertically with a tiny gold bar, forcing them to keep their backs straight and their hands high. The nipple piercing had been pushed through some kind of slotted washer, to which the rawhide cord had been tied.

'Yeah, we use bar piercing here at Bitter Wells. Some farms use rings, others use clips. But we find the clips hurt like hell and come off too easily. If you want we take the bars out when you leave, and the holes will close up naturally over time. Personally I like the way the bars look straight up and down and they're only fifty bucks for the set.'

He held each girl's breast and turned the washer until its slot was in line with the nipple piercing, then he removed the washer. Then he clipped the top of the body harness to the strap ring under Ming's chin and stepped behind her. 'You got three straps to tighten,' he instructed, 'at the chest, the waist, and between the legs. The one between the legs splits in two in the back so that we don't interfere with the tail, and buckles to the bottom of the waist strap.' He demonstrated on Ming as he talked. 'Once the body straps are tight, you pull in their arms with the same straps by using a second buckle. Nothing to remember, really, the straps fall naturally at the pony's biceps and at her elbow. Then you just buckle her wrists to the crotch strap so that their hands don't move around.

He finished up and turned Ming fully around so I could see. The harness was now part of her body.

Jack stepped back and invited me to try it out with Jesse. She moved back when I touched her bare skin, but otherwise there was no reaction as I positioned the straps and tightened them around her.

Jack walked back to the rack and retrieved a lightweight metal rod. It had metal loops at each end. There were two pairs of flat points in the rod where horizontal slots had been cut. 'This is called a nipple bar,' he explained. 'It attaches as so...' He retrieved two small chains from the rack and attached one end to the outside of each girl's mouth bit, then he lifted the rod and attached the chain to the metal loops at each end of the bar. 'It also attaches to the nipples, like this.' He took a firm hold of Ming's breasts and turned then a quarter-turn until the vertical nipple piercing was horizontal and in line with the slot in the bar, then he pushed it through.

When he took his hand away her breast returned to its normal position, locking the bar in place. 'The piercing is impossible to pull out without the use of your hands,' he announced proudly. He stepped back again and gestured for me to do the same to Jesse. I took hold of her breast. I had forgotten how good she felt. Then I turned it as he had done and pushed her nipple piece through the slot. I did the same with the other, noting there was no expression on her face at all.

'The bar keeps their bodies straight when they're running and it allows you to steer,' he explained. Grabbing it in the middle he moved the two girls around the stable until they were standing in front of a small one-man carriage. I could see that both girls were responding immediately and lifting their feet high to his movement of the bar.

'This here is called a drag,' he said. 'It's as light and small as we can make it, but it's still a drag for the ponies compared to running free. Thus the name. We try to give them equal time running with the drag and without so that they don't develop any bad habits.' As he talked he attached the drag's tongue to their harnesses at chest and waist.

'A two-point harness gives them the ability to retain their balance and pull with both their upper and lower body.' Then he attached two thin leather reins to each side of the nipple bar, and finally joined the inside rings of their bits with a short chain.

'All of this is really simple,' he went on with his running instruction. 'When you pull on the rein the steering bar, their nipples, and both mouth bits get pulled in that direction. I guarantee you that the team will also move in that direction to relieve the pressure. Pull back evenly on both when you want them to stop.'

He patted the seat. 'Hop up here, Mr Lowe, and I'll show you.' I did as he said and he handed me the reins. 'Give me a pull to the left.' I pulled on the left rein and both girls immediately turned to that side in response to the pull on their nipples and mouths. I pulled to the right and observed the same reaction. I tried both pulls again and they responded in exactly the same way.

Jack reached over and pulled the buggy whip from its holder on the side of the carriage. 'You shouldn't need to use this on such an easy run, but if they give you any trouble just snap this on their ass or legs. It hurts like hell so use it sparingly. Snapping it over their heads like this,' he demonstrated, 'is the signal to move forward and to go faster.' The girls moved forward instinctively as he demonstrated, and he had to pull the reins to hold them in place. It was amazing actually; they knew it was just a demonstration but their training had also made their responses instinctive. Did they really think of themselves now, at least in part, as ponies?

'If you want to stop along the road be sure to tie their reins to a fence or a tree.' Then he leaned in close and whispered. 'First time out with a new driver and they always try to test them. Keep them on a tight rein and if they really get feisty, unhook them from the carriage and give them a good whipping. Do them both the same, no matter who's at fault. You'll have a better ride tomorrow if you do.'

Then he stood back and said, 'Just follow the dirt road to the right. It takes you around the lake and right back to this spot. You can't get lost. Ming's owner won't be here until next week, so you can have full use of the team while you're here.' He looked at his watch. 'Have them back by five, okay? We like to feed them on a regular schedule. You're welcome to use Ming for sex tonight if you like, but I'm sure you're anxious to get reacquainted with Jesse. Your choice. Or fuck them both if you want.' Out of the corner of my eye I could see Jesse's head turning slightly in our direction, and because of the chain holding their heads together, Ming's head turned at the same time.

'You're all set. See you in a few hours.' Then Jack stepped aside.

I looked at the two pony asses in front of me, tightened up on the reins, and snapped the whip over their heads. They stepped out together at a walk, bending at the waist a little to take up the weight of the carriage. It was amazing; their shod feet sounded exactly like horse hooves.

I tried a few slow turns as we rode down the path. They responded instantly to pulls on the nipple bar just as Jack had said they would. I savored the feel of the reins in my hands; I pulled, they felt pain and turned in the direction I wanted us to go. It was stimulating to have such control. It was also an incredible turn-on to watch their asses move and their leg muscles stretch at each step. They were animals, I thought, beautiful creatures trained to work so that I could ride in comfort. It was getting easier and easier to think of them in this way. In fact, if it wasn't for the case that I wanted desperately to fuck them both, their humanity would have totally left my mind.

I wondered what it would be like to push them faster, but caution won out and I kept them at a walking pace until we were clear of the farm, and then I snapped the whip. They increased their speed to a slow jog. I could see the muscles in their legs and back straining now to take up the increased pull of the drag. I kept it this way for another mile. Sweat dripped off their naked bodies, but they didn't slacken the pace. I had the sense that they could pull all day at this speed.

Suddenly I noticed that Jesse had lost her rhythm. This threw Ming off and the carriage started to swing erratically from one side of the path to the other. I gave Jesse a sharp whack on her ass with the whip, and then another. She corrected her pace, but within half a mile lost it again. I knew what was happening.

I pulled sharply on the right strap and the drag moved off the path. I stepped down and moved to the front of the team. Both girls were breathing heavily, but did not appear to be tired. They were in magnificent shape. I unhooked them from the carriage and led them by their reins to a nearby wooden fence. They followed the pull on their nipples obediently. Ming kept giving Jesse confused glances, but Jesse stared straight down at the ground.

It was a rail fence, maybe four feet high. 'Step up on the bottom rail,' I ordered, but neither girl moved. I threw the reins over the rail and pulled, their nipples stretching painfully. I pulled again and then stepped onto the second rail. 'Bend over the rail.' Again neither girl moved, so I was forced to pull down on the nipple bar to get them to bend. I quickly tied the bar to the bottom rail and then to their ankles. Then I took Ming's right foot and tied it as high as I could to the top rail. Her ass, her legs, and her inner thighs were now fully exposed and immobile. I could see Jesse's left leg moving in anticipation. She expected to be tied in a similar fashion for their punishment.

I found a young sapling, broke off a branch and stripped it of leaves. Then I moved behind Ming and whipped her viciously. She was screaming through the bit. I waited until she was calm and then did it again, and again, and again. By the time I was finished she was writhing in pain.

Jesse, who could feel every stroke and every reaction, was crying as well even though she had not been struck.

I grabbed Jesse's bridle and pulled her face to mine. 'Shall I do it again?' I asked her.

She couldn't speak, but vigorously shook her head. 'If you lose the pace again I'll mount her on a fence rail and whip her raw.' Jesse blinked back the tears and nodded her understanding.

The ride back was easier and faster, with Jesse, who was easily the stronger member of the team, never losing the pace.

A stable boy helped me get the girls out of their harnesses and wiped down. I watched as he washed them down with a gentle hose and dried them off with towels. He treated them as if they were real ponies. The girls responded in the same way, never flinching even when he cleaned inside their vaginas and asses with a padded and oiled rod. It was obvious that the dehumanizing process was part of their total experience.

I tipped him and left.

After a simple dinner with the other guests I returned to the stable and walked to the stall the girls shared. The boy had left them standing naked, chained to the wall. I stepped past Jesse and untied Ming. Then I led her away to my room. I could hear Jesse trying to say something through the bit and stomping her bare feet on the wooden floor.

Every room had an interesting feature for the use of the guests. It was a full size figure of a horse running with its legs fully extended, although the head and rear were missing. There were eye-bolts half-hidden by the false hair along the length of each leg, and a steel head brace rose up at the neck. I put Ming on the horse, pulling her body tight over the frame by using the most extreme eye-bolts. Then I removed her bridle and locked her head in the brace.

I stood back. In the firelight she looked amazing, like a galloping horse. I moved in close, fondling her breasts and her cunt for several minutes, enjoying the feel of her taut, vulnerable body. She responded to my touch and started to push her crotch into the horse, and after a while she came with a gentle shudder.

'She loves you,' she whispered unexpectedly, and I looked at her in surprise.

'CELTs who talk without permission are normally whipped,' I reminded her, the flickering light from the fireplace dancing on her tanned flesh.

'But she loves you,' she repeated.

I grabbed a cane from the umbrella rack by the door and gave her five hard strokes on each ass cheek, and she was inhaling hard through clenched teeth by the time I finished.

'Got anything else to say?' I challenged.

'She love... loves you,' the girl ventured determinedly, despite the pain and discomfort.

I moved in front of her to look into her eyes, moving the cane threateningly. It was clear that I was ready to thrash her again. 'What do you care?' I asked angrily.

'She's my drag partner,' was her enigmatic reply, and somehow that actually made sense to me.

I looked at her for a long minute, and then said, 'Unfortunately she doesn't love me as much as I love her.'

She returned my challenging stare. 'Yes, she does.'

I walked back to the umbrella stand and put the cane back. Then I walked back to the gorgeous girl and pushed my cock into her mouth. The time for talking was finished. She sucked it hard for several minutes, and then I pulled out and moved behind her. I fucked her ass aggressively, and then switched to her cunt. Finally I returned to her mouth and came, and she swallowed avidly and then sucked me dry with enthusiasm.

I left her stretched on the horse and went to bed feeling satisfied, listening to her easy breathing.

In the morning I fucked her again, and then dropped her off at the stable before heading to breakfast without looking into Jesse's stall.

After breakfast Jack was waiting for me in the stable. 'Want to try some sprints this morning?' he asked, and when I agreed, curious, he went to a corner of the stable and returned with a different style of cart.

'This is a racer,' he told me as he moved it into position. 'It's smaller and lighter than those used at the track, but still designed for speed.' He attached it to their harnesses, and then taking the reins in one hand he led the girls outside to the rear of the stable.

'And this is our track,' he said, pointing to a long grassy path that wound around the meadow for maybe a quarter of a mile. 'Keep it slow the first few times around until you get the hang of it, then you can let them go. Try to use the whip as little as possible so they can concentrate on their rhythm, but don't let them slack off either.'

I nodded and snapped the whip. The girls moved out slowly onto the path. I cracked it again and they picked up speed. After two times around I snapped the whip hard again and they moved out at a fast jog. It was easy to keep them on the track, but I could see how important it was that they worked together as we went faster. We went around once that way, then I snapped it again and they started to race. It was amazing to watch their legs pumping in perfect harmony, although Jesse, the strongest of the pair, seemed to be holding back slightly to allow Ming to keep up. But I used the whip on Ming and she picked up her speed to keep up with Jesse's faster pace.

I stopped them after the second fast lap. They were both breathing hard and glistening with sweat, but they were not in any kind of distress. I was amazed at their stamina. I would have had a hard time with such fast laps, even without the racer attached.

What magnificent creatures they were. I waited until their breathing slowed and then glanced over at Jack, who was leaning back on a fence rail. He nodded and I snapped the whip again. This time after a few more fast laps they were noticeably more tired. I needed to use the whip on both girls several times to maintain the pace, and I could tell they were finished racing for the moment.

I stopped the racer in front of Jack. 'Good run,' he said. 'We'll water and rest them and you can take them out again this afternoon. As you can see, we've done a pretty good job with only two weeks' work.' I nodded in enthusiastic agreement.

Later in the afternoon I took them on a long trot, returning to the stable at five. After dinner I went and fetched Ming, and fucked her repeatedly while she rode the horse in my room. Afterwards we slept together, comfortable in each other's arms.

I didn't run the team the next morning, preferring to rest and catch up on a little work. But that afternoon I hitched them up to the drag and ran them at a steady pace for about three miles. Then I stopped to rest by a small pond. I took both girls out of the harness and bridle and allowed them to drink from the pond and cool off in the water while I relaxed against a tree. After some initial shyness they started to fool around like kids. I enjoyed watching them play for a while, and then I stripped off my own clothes and joined them in the cool water.

They hesitated at first, and then Ming splashed me a little. I responded by dunking her and the fun was on. We all enjoyed the time and ended up lying together on the grass. Jesse was playful but reserved, obviously still hurt from the rejection of the prior two evenings.

After a while I rolled Ming onto her back and put on her wrist cuffs, and then I did the same with Jesse, both girls watching me curiously. Then I helped Ming stand up and positioned her under a branch of a nearby oak tree. Attaching the rein to her wrists, I tossed it over the branch and pulled her arms up until she was on tiptoe. Jesse sat up on her knees and watched, intrigue in her eyes, but she didn't say anything. I fetched the buggy whip from the drag and tossed it at her feet.

'Whip her until I tell you to stop,' I ordered. Jesse looked at me with a confused expression, and then shook her head, so I walked over to Ming and raised her further until her toes were off the ground.

'You know what this feels like,' I said. 'Now do as you're told or we can just watch her suffer all afternoon.' Ming was beginning to cry out from the pain. She had heard every word.

'Please, Jess, pleeease, my arms...' Her breathing was labored even after a few seconds in the air.

'Please, Howard, don't make me do this,' Jesse said, but I ignored her and sat down on the ground in a comfortable position to watch Ming suffer. After a few seconds Jesse picked up the whip resignedly and took a position behind her new friend. Then she started to softly lash the girl.

'She can stay up there all day if that's what you want. Now lay it into her properly. I want to see red marks on every inch of her,' I threatened.

'Please, Jess, just do it,' Ming pleaded desperately. 'You're just making it worse.'

So Jesse started to apply the whip with moderate force, which didn't leave much of a mark. She looked over at me and I shook my head, indicating that it wasn't good enough. She began to whip the girl harder, moving methodically down both sides of her body. Jesse was shaking after each stroke and each accompanying scream from the bound and hanging girl, but after a while Ming fell quiet.

'Stop,' I eventually ordered, and Jesse threw the whip to the ground, collapsed and started to cry herself. I let Ming down then took her to the pond and gently washed cool water over her welted body.

'I'm sorry,' I said, and she looked at me with sudden understanding, and nodded.

The ride back was slow, with Ming straining painfully in her harness. Jesse tried to do most of the work, but the drag was designed to be pulled by a team with an even distribution of work, so Ming had to do her share. After a while I stepped down from the drag and walked alongside it.

The stable boy looked at me with disapproval when he saw Ming's beaten body, but he didn't say anything.

I went off to dinner, surprisingly feeling little remorse, then that evening I went to the stable and as usual I approached Ming. The stable boy had applied some soothing lotion to her welts, but it was obvious that she really needed some time to recuperate, so instead I untied Jesse, apparently my second choice, and led her out of the stable to my room.

Once there I strapped her to the horse. She looked magnificent stretched out over the frame. She watched me as I tied her head in place, but I didn't look her in the eyes. Then I closed the lights and got into bed. We both lay awake in the darkness, and I could hear movement and a gentle crying from the horse.

After a while I heard her whisper, so softly I had to strain to hear her. 'Please love me, Master,' she said, repeating it over and over, like a prayer.

I slipped out of bed and stood in front of her. I was naked and my erection was level with her mouth, and she had to lift her head a little to look up into my face.

'Do you accept me as your Master?' I asked in a low voice.

'No,' she replied. 'I don't need to accept you. You are my Master.' It was said simply and it just felt like the truth. I moved my cock closer to her mouth. She stretched forward and was just able to lick the tip, and then I stabbed my hips forward and pushed my cock down her throat. She embraced it as I started to fuck her mouth hard. I could see her moving in rhythm with my thrusts. She came when I came and there were tears in her eyes. I released her from the horse and we slept in each other's arms until morning, when we made exquisite love in the cozy bed.

Then we got up, and after a shower together, I returned her to the stable and went to breakfast.

That day was an easy one for the team, and once again we all enjoyed the pond. Both girls were a little nervous that there would be a repeat of the previous day's unprovoked punishment, but that was good. I preferred a little tension; it helped keep them focused and in line.

The next morning Jesse said her tearful goodbyes to Ming, and we drove home.

CHAPTER TWELVE

Our time at Bitter Wells defined our relationship.

Jesse moved into my bedroom, maintaining hers as 'private space', which I respected. She has also gone back to school under the guise of being my live-in girlfriend. Not that I'm concerned anymore about making her status as a CELT public. In fact, I still can't believe that that was once my highest priority. Jesse's just more comfortable keeping that part of our lives private.

We have our times of tender love as well as our times of bondage and pain. In between is an easy friendship. It's not the friendship of friends - that is, equals, sharing common experience; it's the friendship of lovers - a kind of constant non-sexual intercourse where one of us is naturally subordinate to the other. Jesse seems to thrive in it. I don't know why exactly; I just know that she does.

Maybe it's what she said; this kind of relationship is a complex soup of emotions. All I know is that it's beyond ordinary love, way beyond. If you can imagine!

Her contract ends in six months. I'm saving my money.

www.ingramcontent.com/pod-product-compliance
Lightning Source LLC
Chambersburg PA
CBHW071220130626
46555CB00004B/1783